SOMEBODY'S WATCHING ME

Some secrets never remain buried

SHEKELLE A. BAZEMORE

MARLIN L. COOKS

This book is being dedicated to Marlin Lee Cooks.

Marlin, you were an inspiration and a ray of light to so many. Although you are no longer with us, your kindred spirit, your creativity, your compassionate soul, and your kind heart will always be missed. We will forever cherish the time spent with you. Until we meet again, We Love You!

CONTENTS

PART ONE - SECRETS UNKNOWN   1

CHAPTER ONE.   2

CHAPTER TWO.   9

CHAPTER THREE.   23

CHAPTER FOUR.   34

CHAPTER FIVE.   42

CHAPTER SIX.   49

PART TWO - BATTLING WITH THE TRUTH   57

CHAPTER SEVEN.   58

CHAPTER EIGHT.   68

CHAPTER NINE.   77

CHAPTER TEN.   85

CHAPTER ELEVEN.   94

CHAPTER TWELVE.   101

CHAPTER THIRTEEN.   108

CHAPTER FOURTEEN.   116

CHAPTER FIFTEEN.   126

CHAPTER SIXTEEN.   138

CHAPTER SEVENTEEN.   143

PART THREE - PATH TO NEW BEGINNINGS   147

CHAPTER EIGHTEEN.   148

CHAPTER NINETEEN.   155

CHAPTER TWENTY.   161

CHAPTER TWENTY-ONE.   167

CHAPTER TWENTY-TWO.   174

CHAPTER TWENTY-THREE.   184

CHAPTER TWENTY-FOUR.   191

CHAPTER TWENTY-FIVE.   198

SHEKELLE A. BAZEMORE & MARLIN L. COOKS

PART ONE - SECRETS UNKNOWN

CHAPTER ONE.

B eyond the broken harbor hung the cold light of day. Ashes swirling in the wind. The echoes of those passed filtering through the boardwalk asserted itself... *The memory of those beloved was locked in the smoke and the ashen fibers, of course, it meant life... And yet the past it constructed...* rising and falling in pitch and falling away as the memories moved on, the secrets of someone dear following with them.

Nikki Lewis stood by the quay; her gaze fixed upon the tranquil expanse of water. This hallowed ground, where she had bid her late husband George farewell with tear-stained cheeks, had become a refuge in her bereavement. It beckoned her with the promise of solace and whispered memories, and so she found herself drawn to its embrace time and time again.

Lost in her thoughts, Nikki was startled when a stranger materialized beside her, his presence an unwelcome intrusion upon her private sanctuary. The man, in his late thirties, possessed an awkward smile that failed to reach his eyes. There was an air of unease surrounding him, an unsettling energy that caused her heart to flutter uneasily in her chest.

He turned his gaze towards the water, seemingly unaffected by the discomfort he had imposed upon her, and remarked, "Beautiful day, isn't it?"

Nikki, her polite smile masking her unease, nodded in agreement. She yearned for the conversation to dissolve into silence, for the stranger to recognize the sanctity of this place and leave her in her solitude. She was not accustomed to engaging with strangers, especially in a space that held such profound significance for her. But the man persisted, his inquiries probing deeper into her life, encroaching upon her personal boundaries. He questioned her frequent visits to the quay, her residency in the area, and other seemingly harmless details.

Each question intensified the knot of discomfort within Nikki's core. She couldn't shake the unsettling feeling that this encounter was not a mere coincidence. Was he observing her from afar, patiently biding his time until she was vulnerable and alone?

Her mind swirled with cautionary whispers, her late husband's voice echoing in her memory, reminding her of the dangers that lurked in the shadows.

Her resolve solidified, and Nikki decided it was time to extricate herself from this disconcerting encounter. She offered a brief, polite farewell, hoping the hint of her departure would be enough to prompt his retreat. "I'm sorry, but I really must be going," she stated, her voice gentle yet firm. "It was nice to meet you."

The stranger's smile widened, betraying no hint of his true intentions, as he nodded in acquiescence. "Nice to meet you too. Take care."

With a sense of urgency, Nikki walked away briskly, placing distance between herself and the disconcerting stranger. She sought solace in the rhythmic cadence of her hurried footsteps, trying to shake off the unease that clung to her like an invisible shroud. Doubt gnawed at her, tempting her to dismiss her concerns as paranoia, yet an instinctual wariness urged her to heed the warning signs. Something felt amiss, a lingering shadow that defied easy explanation.

Nikki sat aboard the subway, lost in the depths of her thoughts. Her visit to the harbor, the very spot where she had scattered her husband's ashes almost a year ago, had left a bittersweet imprint on her soul. The place held countless memories, fragments of a love that had flourished amidst the sea breeze and the dancing waves. But now, it served as a stark reminder of the profound absence that had settled within her.

As the subway train carried her homeward, Nikki grappled with a whirlwind of emotions. Gratitude swelled within her for the precious moments she had shared with her beloved husband, but the weight of sorrow bore heavily upon her heart. Images of their past intertwined with the present, a tapestry of joy and grief that unfolded relentlessly. Tears welled in her eyes, cascading down her cheeks, as she navigated the sea of commuters, the anonymity of the crowded subway offering little solace in her solitude.

In her vulnerable state, Nikki's attention was drawn to a man who had fixed his gaze upon her. He sat across the aisle, his eyes holding an intensity that sent shivers down her spine. The weight of his scrutiny made her skin prickle, igniting a flicker of unease within her. She sought refuge in a fleeting distraction, averting her gaze, but she could still feel his piercing eyes upon her, an unwelcome intrusion into her private realm of sorrow.

Attempting to reclaim her composure, Nikki dabbed at her tear-stained cheeks, her fingers trembling slightly. Yet, she couldn't escape the unsettling sensation that the man's penetrating gaze had seen beyond her facade, witnessing her raw vulnerability. Her heart yearned for him to look away, to release her from this discomfiting scrutiny. But as the subway rattled onward, he rose from his seat, a determined resolve etched upon his features, and began to make his way toward her.

Her pulse quickened, apprehension coiling within her, as she silently pleaded for him to pass her by. But fate had other plans, as the man halted before her, his voice tender and laced with genuine concern.

"Are you Okay?" he inquired his words like a gentle breeze that brushed against the fragile petals of her wounded heart.

Nikki's guard wavered; the unease momentarily eclipsed by the sincerity she detected in his voice. A sliver of vulnerability found solace in his genuine concern, inviting her to lower her defenses ever so slightly. Yet, caution still danced upon the precipice of her consciousness, reminding her of the world's treacherous twists and turns.

A flicker of gratitude passed through Nikki's eyes as she met his gaze. She considered his question, grappling with the complexity of her emotions, unsure of how much to reveal. In this fleeting encounter, she sensed a fleeting connection, a shared understanding of the human struggle.

"I... I'm going through a difficult time," she murmured, her voice laced with a mix of vulnerability and caution.

The man nodded; his expression filled with empathy. "I'm sorry to hear that," he replied softly, his words a gentle balm to her wounded spirit. "If there's anything I can do, please let me know. Sometimes, it helps to share the burden."

Nikki's guarded heart remained tentative, her past experiences guiding her steps with measured caution. But in that fleeting moment, amidst the chaos of the subway and the weight of her grief, she recognized a glimmer of humanity, an unexpected connection that offered a brief respite from her solitary sorrow. And with a grateful smile, she whispered her appreciation, allowing herself to momentarily embrace the solace offered by the kindness of a stranger.

"Hello again. I hope I'm not bothering you, but I couldn't help but notice that you seem upset. Is everything okay?"

Nikki tried to brush off the stranger's concern, insisting that she was fine and just needed some time alone. But the man didn't seem to take no for an answer. He sat down opposite her and began to make small talk, asking her where she was headed and if she lived in the area.

"I'm just heading home to... Woodley Grove," Nikki replied curtly, hoping he would take the hint and leave her alone.

"I live near there too," the man said with a smile. "I'm actually on my way to meet some friends for dinner. Would you like to join us?"

Nikki was taken aback by the man's invitation. She had never met him before, and the thought of joining him and his friends for dinner seemed a little strange. But at the same time, she appreciated his kindness and the distraction it might provide from her own thoughts.

"Thank you for the offer, but I think I'll just head home," she said politely.

The man didn't seem to take the hint, however, and continued to make small talk with her. He asked her about her job and her hobbies, and even shared some stories from his own life. Nikki found herself slowly opening up to him, sharing bits and pieces of her own life and her memories of her husband.

As the subway neared her stop, Nikki began to gather her things, ready to make a quick exit. But the man stood up with her, insisting on walking her to the door.

"Thank you for the company," Nikki said, as they reached the door. "But I really do need to go now."

The man smiled warmly at her. "Of course. I hope you have a good evening, and maybe we'll run into each other again sometime."

Nikki stepped off the subway.

CHAPTER TWO.

Nikki walked home, still feeling shaken from her encounter with the stranger. It was early evening, and the sun was starting to set, casting a warm orange glow over the streets. The vibrant colors that would typically bring her joy now seemed muted, almost mocking her current state of mind. She kept glancing over her shoulder, paranoid that someone might be following her, but she didn't see anyone.

Despite her efforts to stay alert, her mind kept wandering back to the stranger on the subway. The memory of his piercing eyes and the way he seemed to study her every move replayed in her mind like a haunting melody. She couldn't shake the feeling that he had been watching her, even after she had left the train. She tried to push the thought out of her mind, telling herself that she was just being paranoid, but the unease persisted like an unwelcome shadow.

Finally, after what felt like an eternity, Nikki reached her front door. Her trembling hands fumbled with the lock as she struggled to insert the key into its rightful place. Her nerves were frayed, and the physical task became an impossible challenge. She felt tears prick at the corners of her eyes, and she took a deep, shuddering breath, trying to calm herself down.

The weight of the day's events crashed down on her as frustration mingled with fear. Every small setback seemed magnified, reminding her of the vulnerability she felt in that subway car. Her husband's absence loomed larger than ever, his once-reassuring presence now an unfillable void. She had relied on him for strength and security, but his sudden departure from her life left her exposed to the uncertainties of the world.

After what seemed like an eternity, Nikki finally managed to unlock the door and stumble into her home. The familiar scent of comfort and familiarity embraced her, providing a brief respite from the chaos outside. She quickly locked the door behind her, feeling the weight of the world lifting off her shoulders. It was a small victory in a day marred by unease.

Collapsing in a heap by the doorway, Nikki let the tears flow freely. Her body trembled with the release of pent-up emotions as grief surged through her like a relentless tide.

Memories of her husband flooded her thoughts, their laughter echoing in her mind, the touch of his hand fading but not forgotten. She thought about the life they had built together, the dreams they had shared, and the plans they had made. It was a pain that never seemed to go away, no matter how much time passed.

As Nikki sat there, lost in her thoughts, the emotions intensified. The magnitude of her loss became unbearable, and she longed for a moment of solace. The world seemed so vast and indifferent; her solitude amplified by the silence of her empty home. She yearned for someone to understand, someone to share her burden, but the weight of grief was hers alone to bear.

Eventually, the tears subsided, leaving Nikki exhausted and emotionally drained. She found solace in the stillness of the house, the quiet providing a temporary reprieve from the chaos outside. Gathering her strength, she slowly rose to her feet, determined to face the challenges that lay ahead. The encounter with the stranger had reminded her of her vulnerability, but it had also ignited a flicker of resilience within her.

Grief was a relentless adversary, gripping Nikki's heart and soul like a vice. It lurked in the corners of her mind, an ever-present specter that haunted her waking hours. The path through grief was an enigma, twisting and turning, with no clear direction. It was a tempest, unleashing torrents of emotions upon her without warning.

Yet Nikki was no stranger to the treacherous terrain of grief. She traversed its intricate labyrinth with a tenacity that defied its oppressive weight. She understood that healing was not a linear march, but a dance of ebbs and flows. On some days, the pain threatened to engulf her, a tidal wave crashing upon her fragile shores. But amidst the darkness, a flicker of hope would emerge, reminding her of life's potential for beauty and joy.

Grief, she realized, was not a monotonous dirge of tears and sorrow. It was a kaleidoscope of emotions, swirling and colliding, at times in perfect harmony, and at others in dissonant chaos. It was the poignant recollection of shared laughter, the ache for another touch, another conversation. It was the simultaneous longing for both the absence and the presence of loved ones—a testament to the depth of her love.

Amidst the tempest, Nikki sought solace in the most ordinary of moments. She found comfort in the ritual of brewing a cup of tea, its warmth seeping into her being, easing the burden that weighed upon her shoulders. She sought refuge in the arms of her loved ones, finding solace in their mere presence, a salve for her wounded spirit. And within the pages of books, she discovered narratives that mirrored the indomitable spirit of humanity, reminding her of the resilience that resided within her own soul.

Nikki walked through the silent halls of her empty house; her steps muffled by the weight of grief that clung to her like a second skin. The rooms echoed with memories, and each corner seemed to harbor a ghost of the life she once had. The walls, once adorned with family photographs and laughter, now stared back at her, barren and desolate.

She traced her fingers along the familiar contours of the furniture, her touch seeking solace in the coldness of the wood. It had been a year since George's passing, but the wound in her heart remained fresh, a constant ache that refused to subside. Time was supposed to heal, they said, but it felt like an empty promise, a cruel illusion.

The house was a testament to their shared history, a repository of love and happiness. Every object held a story, every room a chapter of their intertwined lives. But now, the memories were bittersweet, tinged with the sorrow of loss. The laughter that once resounded on these walls had been replaced by an oppressive silence.

In the living room, Nikki sank into the well-worn armchair, the fabric absorbing her weariness. She gazed at the empty space on the wall where their wedding portrait had once hung, George's warm smile frozen in time. How could a home, once filled with love and laughter, become so void of life? It felt like a betrayal as if the universe had conspired to snatch away her happiness.

Her mind traveled back to the days when George's presence had filled every room, his laughter a melody that danced through the air. The memories were vivid, like scenes from a movie playing in her mind. The smell of his cologne, the touch of his hand, the sound of his voice whispering sweet nothings in her ear—it all felt so tangible, yet so far away.

Tears welled up in Nikki's eyes, threatening to spill over. She fought against them, refusing to succumb to the overwhelming grief that engulfed her. But grief had a way of creeping in, insidious and relentless, until it wrapped its tendrils around her heart, squeezing the life out of her.

She rose from the armchair, her steps heavy as she moved toward the bedroom they had once shared. The room felt like a sanctuary, a shrine to their love. The bed, now empty and cold, held the imprint of their bodies, a stark reminder of the intimacy they had shared.

Nikki sat on the edge of the bed, her fingers trailing along the smooth sheets. She closed her eyes, immersing herself in the memories that swirled around her. Their whispered conversations in the late hours of the night, the laughter that erupted from beneath the covers, the shared dreams, and aspirations—they all seemed like distant echoes, fading into the abyss of her loneliness.

In this emptiness, Nikki found herself grappling with the enormity of her loss. The weight of her grief threatened to engulf her, to pull her into the depths of despair. But she knew that she couldn't stay lost in this labyrinth of sorrow forever. She had to find a way to navigate through the darkness and carve a new path for herself.

With a deep breath, Nikki rose from the bed, determined to honor George's memory in her own way. She would carry him within her, cherishing the love they had shared. The house may be empty, but her heart would always be filled with the echoes of their love. And in time, she would find a way to transform her grief into strength, to forge a new life out of the ashes of her pain.

Nikki made her way to the kitchen, the heaviness of grief clinging to her like a shroud. She craved solace, something to ease the ache in her heart. The familiar ritual of making coffee provided a fleeting respite from the weight of her sorrow.

As she patiently waited for the water to boil, she gazed out of the window, watching as the raindrops tapped rhythmically against the glass. The sound, a soothing melody amid her turmoil, offered a momentary escape. The world outside seemed distant and blurred, the rain acting as a veil between her and the harsh realities of life.

Lost in her thoughts, Nikki was momentarily transported to a place of tranquility. But as she turned to pour the coffee into her cup, a flicker of movement caught her attention. Her eyes darted to the corner of the room, where a fleeting shadow danced against the wall. A surge of unease coursed through her veins, disrupting the fragile calm she had found.

She attempted to dismiss the sight as a figment of her restless imagination, a consequence of the tension that had plagued her throughout the day. Yet, the disquiet remained, refusing to be ignored.

Slowly, apprehension weighing her every step, Nikki turned her gaze back to the corner. There, partially obscured by the cloak of shadows, stood a figure. It was George, or at least an apparition of his youthful self that had begun to haunt her waking hours.

A gasp escaped Nikki's lips, her grip on the teapot faltering. Hot water spilled onto the countertop; its scalding touch momentarily forgotten. George took a step closer, concern etching lines of worry across his face.

"Nikki, are you alright? What's troubling you?" he inquired, his hand reaching out as if to offer solace.

Nikki recoiled, her mind awash with uncertainty. Was this a manifestation of her deepest desires or a cruel trick played by her own mind? She shook her head, desperately attempting to convince herself that it was nothing more than a hallucination.

"I'm fine, George. Just a trick of the mind," she replied, her voice quivering, her words echoing with fragile conviction.

But George remained a steadfast presence in the corner of the kitchen, his eyes brimming with concern. A single tear traced a path down Nikki's cheek, her emotions threatening to overwhelm her. Collapsing onto a nearby chair, she surrendered to the weight of her grief, feeling as though the walls of her fragile world were closing in.

"I miss you so much," she whispered, her voice barely a murmur, yet heavy with the weight of her longing.

George approached her, his steps were purposeful yet gentle. He knelt beside her, his hand finding its place upon her shoulder, a touch of comfort amidst the storm of emotions. Nikki leaned into him, seeking solace in his intangible presence as if the memory of his warmth could chase away the cold tendrils of loneliness.

"It's alright, Nikki. I am still here, in your memories and in the depths of your heart. You do not have to face this journey alone," he murmured, his voice a tender caress against her pain.

Closing her eyes, Nikki allowed herself to breathe, to absorb the soothing reassurances that George offered. She knew deep down that she needed to confront her hallucinations, to seek the guidance of those who could help her navigate the labyrinth of her own mind. But for now, in this fragile moment, having George by her side, even if only in her thoughts, brought a modicum of solace.

Nikki's mind wandered back to that fateful day, etched in her memory like a relentless scar. It was a day that began with mundane routines, oblivious to the seismic shift that awaited her. George, her beloved husband, had decided to take a break from his artistic pursuits, his head throbbing with a persistent ache. He mentioned a quick trip to the supermarket, a routine errand that would forever alter the course of their lives.

Little did she know that those parting words, "See you soon, little bird," would become an echo, a haunting reminder of a farewell that held more weight than she could have fathomed. It was a tender endearment, spoken with affection and a sense of familiarity that now reverberated through the depths of her being.

The day unraveled with cruel swiftness. The sun cast its gentle rays upon their home, blissfully unaware of the impending tragedy. And then, there came a knock at the door —a seemingly innocuous disturbance that would unleash an avalanche of anguish. Nikki, unsuspecting, opened the door to the somber faces of uniformed officers, their eyes clouded with empathy, and hearts heavy with the burden of delivering devastating news.

The world shattered in an instant. Reality splintered, and Nikki found herself crumbling under the weight of unbearable grief. Her knees gave way, and she sank to the floor as if surrendering to the enormity of the loss. Words failed her, drowned in a sea of tears that flowed unchecked. In that vulnerable moment, she became one with her pain, her anguish becoming a primal force that consumed her.

The officers stood, their presence offering silent but tangible support. They understood the gravity of the moment, the fragile threads that held Nikki's shattered world together. Their words of condolence were a mere whisper against the cacophony of grief that enveloped her, but their presence spoke volumes.

Hours merged into an endless blur as Nikki grappled with the stark reality of George's sudden departure. The once-familiar spaces of their home now seemed imbued with a haunting emptiness, each room a stark reminder of the life they had shared. The laughter that once echoed through the halls now hung heavy in the air, mingling with the silent tears that stained her cheeks.

In the depths of her despair, Nikki clung to the memories, the fragments of a life forever altered. She retraced their steps, reliving their moments of joy and tenderness. The brushstrokes of George's artistry adorned the walls, bearing witness to his creativity and passion. Each stroke whispered of dreams unfulfilled, of a future that would never materialize.

Nikki sat on the edge of her cozy couch, her fingers tightly gripping the phone as her mind raced with thoughts of the stranger who had shown up and attempted to follow her from the subway. The unsettling encounter had left her shaken, and she found herself seeking solace in her sister's voice.

"Hi, Kayla," Nikki greeted, her voice quivering slightly with remnants of fear. "No, I'm fine. Just a little shaken up."

There was a brief pause at the other end of the line, and Nikki could almost hear genuine concern lacing her sister's voice. "Are you sure? I know the anniversary is approaching, and it's a lot to handle on your own."

Nikki's defenses immediately went up, her independent nature kicking in. "I'm sure, Kayla. I'm a grown woman; I can handle myself."

Kayla didn't back down, her love for her sister overpowering any resistance. "That may be true, but have you considered seeing a counselor? Talking to someone might help you process everything."

Nikki released a deep sigh, realizing her sister had touched on a sensitive topic. She knew Kayla meant well, but she was reluctant to admit that she might need professional assistance. "I don't need a counselor, Kayla. I'm fine."

Kayla persisted, her voice gentle yet insistent. "Nikki, seeking help is not a sign of weakness. We all need support sometimes, especially during difficult times like these."

A lump formed in Nikki's throat, the weight of her emotions becoming too burdensome to bear alone. She recognized the truth in her sister's words. However, she was apprehensive about confronting the pain and reliving the memories that counseling might unearth. "Okay, fine. Maybe I'll think about it."

Kayla sounded relieved, her voice reflecting a mix of hope and concern. "That's all,

I'm asking, Nikki. I just want you to take care of yourself."

A soft smile tugged at Nikki's lips; her heart warmed by her sister's unwavering concern. "Thanks, Kayla. I appreciate it."

Kayla's tone softened, infused with love and tenderness. "Of course. And remember, if you need anything, just let me know."

"I will," Nikki promised, her voice filled with gratitude. "And Kayla, take care of yourself too. I love you."

"I love you too, Nikki," Kayla replied, her voice betraying a hint of emotion. "We'll get through this together."

Nikki ended the call and sat in contemplative silence, allowing the weight of their conversation to settle upon her.

She knew that Kayla was right — she needed to take care of herself, not just for her own well-being but also for the sake of her loving family. However, Nikki couldn't deny the gnawing uncertainty that accompanied the thought of facing her pain alone.

She glanced at a family portrait displayed on the nearby shelf, a reminder of the love and support that surrounded her. Nikki realized that seeking help didn't equate to weakness; rather, it was a testament to her strength and resilience in the face of adversity. With renewed determination, she made a silent promise to herself to confront her fears and explore the path to healing.

SHEKELLE A. BAZEMORE & MARLIN L. COOKS

CHAPTER THREE.

N ikki found herself once again caught in the grip of her vivid hallucinations. George materialized before her, his youthful visage radiating warmth and familiarity. In this ethereal realm, he held her with tenderness, enveloping her in an embrace that promised solace and safety.

Her mind surrendered to the illusion, allowing herself to be swept away by the ephemeral fantasy. She nestled into his embrace, her body instinctively seeking the comfort it had yearned for since his untimely departure. For a fleeting moment, the weight of her grief seemed to lift, and a sense of serenity settled upon her like a fragile butterfly perched upon a delicate flower.

But as quickly as the vision enveloped her, reality shattered the illusion, thrusting her back into the cold embrace of the present. She blinked her eyes, adjusting to the starkness of her surroundings, and found herself bereft of the solace she had briefly tasted. George, the embodiment of her deepest desires, had vanished, leaving only a void in his wake.

Nikki stood alone, the emptiness around her echoing the emptiness within. The remnants of the hallucination lingered; a phantom sensation of his touch still imprinted upon her skin. But it was just a mirage, an echo of the love that once intertwined their lives.

Her heart ached with a renewed intensity, the absence of his physical presence becoming a tangible weight upon her soul. She yearned for the moments that would never come to pass, the conversations left unspoken, the laughter left unshared. The illusion had only magnified the void, leaving her grasping at intangible fragments of what once was.

In the silence of the room, Nikki confronted the harsh reality of her grief. It was a solitary journey, a path she had to navigate without the physical presence of the one who had held her heart. She clung to the memories, the whispers of their shared past, desperate to keep his spirit alive within her.

But as her hallucinations persisted, Nikki understood that they were both a gift and a curse. In those fleeting moments of illusion, George became a lifeline, a temporary respite from the overwhelming weight of her sorrow. Yet, each time the vision dissipated; the stark reminder of her solitary existence crashed upon her with renewed force.

She took a deep breath, drawing strength from the depths of her pain. She knew that her journey through grief would be punctuated by these bittersweet encounters, these delicate dances with a phantom love. And while they could never replace the tangible presence of George, they offered a brief respite, a reminder of the love that once bloomed in their shared existence.

Nikki wiped away the tears that clung to her cheeks, summoning her resilience once more. She would continue to face her visions, to confront the specter of loss that haunted her. In this dance between reality and illusion, she would find the courage to embrace the fleeting moments of solace, while navigating the unforgiving terrain of her grief.

Alone, yet not entirely alone, Nikki forged ahead. She carried George's memory within her, his spirit forever intertwined with her own. And as she emerged from the ephemeral embrace of her hallucination, she vowed to honor their love by seeking solace in the present, cherishing the memories that would forever guide her through the labyrinth of her grief.

Nikki's heart sank as she realized the fleeting nature of the apparition. The vision of George, however vivid, was just an illusion, a manifestation of her longing and grief. She couldn't rely on these hallucinations to bring her solace or guide her forward.

She rose from the bath, water cascading from her body as she wrapped herself in a towel. Her reflection in the mirror seemed to hold a hint of determination, a spark of resilience flickering within her eyes. She knew that she couldn't keep waiting for George to appear in her dreams or visions. She had to find a way to move forward, to redefine her life without him physically by her side.

Gradually, the fog of grief began to lift, revealing glimpses of a future that was both uncertain and promising. Nikki learned to honor her memories of George without being defined solely by her loss. She carried him within her, not as a burden, but as a reminder of the love they had shared and the strength that resided within her.

Nikki slipped beneath the covers, her body sinking into the soft embrace of the mattress. The weight of the day's burdens clung to her like a second skin, pressing against her weary bones. She closed her eyes, but the darkness offered no respite from the relentless storm brewing within. The echoes of the dream still reverberated through her mind, an unsettling symphony of doubts and regrets. Sleep, that elusive sanctuary, remained just beyond her reach, its ethereal tendrils slipping through her fingers. As the night pressed on, Nikki lay in the shrouded embrace of her bed, grappling with the ghosts of her past, searching for solace in the unyielding darkness.

Nikki's dream unraveled like a twisted tapestry, entwining memories, and emotions in a tumultuous dance. The George that visited her slumber was not a mere specter, but a vivid projection of the man she had loved, his essence etched deep within her consciousness.

In the dream, George sat before her, his smile etched in every line of her imagination, his words forever engraved in her mind. She struggled to grasp the enigma of his presence, the way he had transformed into a living memory, both elusive and palpable.

He had possessed a stubborn streak that was undeniable. But such was the nature of handsome and talented men. On his workdays, his tone could be curt, his demeanor cynical, as if he had little patience for the follies of others. Yet, beneath that facade, a playful and romantic soul resided. He was a man of complexity, a puzzle that should not have fallen under anyone's spell. And yet, they had fallen, completely, for each other.

In her dream, George reclined in his chair, his gaze fixed upon her as he posed a question. "What are you going to do?" he inquired, his voice echoing in her mind.

Confused, Nikki responded, "Do about what?"

"She won't stop," George insisted, his words carrying an undercurrent of concern.

"She was defending herself," Nikki countered, a note of conviction lacing her voice.

George shook his head feebly, a gesture that spoke volumes. Rising from his seat, he began to walk away, beckoning her to follow. With a mixture of curiosity and trepidation, Nikki trailed after him, for what other choice did she have? In this dream realm, she yearned to awaken, yet equally longed to witness the path George would lead her down.

Their journey led them to the place of his passing, a scene filled with haunting familiarity. Nikki gazed upon his lifeless body, a rush of helplessness surging through her. Beside him lay a knife, nestled in a pool of crimson, a vivid symbol of the tragic event. In reality, she had hidden the weapon, obscuring the truth. But in the realm of dreams, the truth shimmered with vivid clarity.

George's voice broke the silence, laden with a tinge of regret. "Could I have done anything differently?" he questioned, a sense of vulnerability creeping into his words.

Nikki's response came swift and resolute, borne from a place of hurt and wisdom. "You could have seen her for what she truly was," she declared, her voice trembling with the weight of her revelation.

The dream wavered, its fragile thread unraveling, and Nikki felt herself teetering on the precipice of wakefulness. George's figure faded into the ether, leaving her alone with her thoughts, entangled in the complexity of her emotions.

She awoke, her body drenched in sweat, her heart pounding within her chest. The dream lingered; its impact seared into her consciousness. It was a reminder of the tangled web of their past, of the choices and actions that had brought them to this point.

Nikki's heart pounded against her chest, its erratic rhythm reverberating through her body as she jolted awake from a restless slumber. Three in the morning. The room was cloaked in darkness, broken only by the feeble glow of the streetlights seeping through the curtains. She strained her ears, hoping to dismiss the sound as remnants of a haunting dream, but the persistent knocking persisted, relentless in its urgency.

With a mix of trepidation and curiosity, Nikki swung her legs over the edge of the bed, the cold wooden floor beneath her feet jolting her awake. She glanced at the empty space beside her, half-expecting to see George's familiar silhouette, his voice of reason to guide her through this strange awakening. But the figure that stood before her was nothing more than a figment of her imagination, an echo of her longing.

George's ghostly form lingered in the doorway, his eyes pleading with her, warning her of impending danger. But Nikki, fueled by a mix of adrenaline and a stubborn curiosity, chose to ignore the ethereal apparition and embarked on a perilous journey toward the source of the disturbance.

Her bare feet grazed the frigid floorboards as she traversed the dimly lit landing, her footsteps muted by the weight of the hour. Every creak and groan of the old house seemed to reverberate through her soul, a symphony of unease that accompanied her descent. Shadows danced and swayed along the walls, casting an eerie backdrop to the unfolding scene.

As Nikki reached the bottom of the stairs, her trembling hand grasped the worn wooden banister, her knuckles turning pale beneath the strain. The knocking grew louder, resonating through the hollow corridors of her home. She braced herself, her mind a tempest of conflicting emotions, and finally mustered the courage to confront the unknown.

"Who's there?" she called out, her voice a frail whisper, strained with a blend of anxiety and defiance.

A muffled voice responded from the other side, its tone laden with desperation and longing. "I'm looking for my dad," it pleaded, the words tinged with youthful innocence.

A surge of confusion and disbelief washed over Nikki. There were no children in her home, no fathers to be found within its solitary walls. But the relentless stranger's insistence pierced through her skepticism, pushing her to confront the enigma that stood on the precipice of her existence.

Her gaze darted towards the baseball bat, a makeshift guardian standing steadfast by the doorway. The instinct for self-preservation urged her to grasp its solid weight, to wield it as a shield against the unknown. With cautious deliberation, she wrapped her fingers around the worn handle, it's comforting familiarity providing a semblance of courage.

Summoning her resolve, Nikki turned the key in the lock, the mechanical click slicing through the tension that hung in the air. The door creaked open, revealing the abyss beyond. She took a deep breath, her heart pounding against her chest like a war drum and slowly stepped into the threshold, her grip tightening on the bat.

The moonlight cast a pale glow upon the figure before her, a silhouette shrouded in darkness. Fear and determination clashed within Nikki's mind as she confronted the unexpected visitor. The world seemed to hold its breath; the weight of the moment suspended in time.

And as the door swung open, revealing the truth that lay concealed in the shadows, Nikki braced herself for whatever awaited her, the haunting echoes of George's warning fading into the recesses of her memory.

Nikki stood behind the closed door, the soft hum of the evening settling around her. She had just settled into her new home, a place of solace and healing after the storm of revelations that had shaken her world. As she contemplated her next steps, a knock interrupted her thoughts.

Startled, Nikki cautiously approached the door, peering through the peephole to catch a glimpse of the visitor on the other side. The dimly lit hallway revealed a man, his face obscured by the shadows cast by the flickering lights overhead. He seemed familiar, though she couldn't find out where she had seen him before.

The man spoke, his voice filled with a mix of hope and uncertainty. "Excuse me, ma'am. Is my father home? I was hoping to see him."

Nikki hesitated, her mind racing to find an explanation. Her heart told her that something was amiss, that this encounter held a deeper significance. The air crackled with an unspoken tension, a sense that this interaction held the key to unlocking a hidden truth.

Gathering her resolve, Nikki replied in a steady voice, "I'm sorry, but there's no one here with children. You must have the wrong address."

The man's eyes narrowed, his brows furrowing with insistence. "No, I'm sure this is the right place. I need to find my father. It's important."

Something about his unwavering determination unsettled Nikki. It triggered a nagging suspicion, a faint echo of the past that threatened to shatter the fragile peace she had found. Despite her apprehension, she held her ground, refusing to be swayed by his persistence.

"I assure you, there is no one here with that description. You should leave," she urged, her voice tinged with a mix of caution and urgency.

The man's expression softened, a glimmer of apology shining through his eyes. "I'm sorry to disturb you. I must have made a mistake. Thank you for your time."

As he turned to leave, Nikki's curiosity got the best of her. She couldn't let this encounter slip away without attempting to unravel its mystery. She quietly slipped ajar the door, peeping through the narrow opening, hoping to catch a glimpse of the man's identity before he disappeared into the night.

However, her efforts were in vain. The darkness swallowed him whole, reducing his figure to a mere silhouette. The dim glow of distant streetlights offered little insight, obscuring his features, and leaving Nikki with more questions than answers.

CHAPTER FOUR.

The soft light of morning filtered through Nikki's window, casting a gentle glow upon the room. As she sat by the sill, her gaze fixed on the world outside, she yearned for a return to normalcy. The neighborhood stirred with life, the distant laughter of children, the chirping of birds, and the rhythmic footsteps of passersby. It all felt like a distant echo of a reality she longed to reclaim.

Lost in her thoughts, Nikki imagined a time when she would fully emerge from the cocoon of grief, when she would once again be an active participant in the vibrant tapestry of life. The notion seemed both daunting and enticing, a delicate balance between healing and embracing the unknown.

Just as her mind wandered through the possibilities that lay ahead, a sudden commotion outside pulled her attention back to the present. Through the windowpane, she glimpsed a young girl and a hooded man engaged in a heated argument on the manicured lawn. Their voices carried on the breeze, filled with tension and frustration.

The girl, her eyes brimming with defiance, flung her arms in exasperation before turning away, striding off with determination etched into her every step. Meanwhile, the hooded man, his features obscured by the shadow cast by his hood, momentarily glanced upward. Though Nikki couldn't discern his face, an unsettling shiver ran down her spine, as if their eyes had briefly met.

Instinctively, Nikki's mind raced with questions. Who were they, and what had transpired between them? The air seemed charged with an unspoken weight, an invisible thread connecting her to this moment of discord. She couldn't shake the feeling that she had inadvertently stumbled upon a fragment of a larger narrative—one that echoed the struggles and secrets that had defined her own journey.

As the hooded man turned away, blending into the background of the bustling neighborhood, Nikki couldn't shake the unease that settled upon her. She wondered about the girl, the lines etched upon her face, the fire in her eyes. What battles had she fought, and what demons had she encountered?

Deep within Nikki's heart, a seed of empathy sprouted. She recognized the familiar yearning for solace, the relentless pursuit of truth and understanding. It was a shared quest, one that bound them together, despite the barriers of time and circumstance.

Drawing a steadying breath, Nikki vowed to remain vigilant, to be attuned to the whispers of disquiet that echoed through the neighborhood. It was a reminder that her own journey was interconnected with the lives around her, and that the path to healing required not only personal strength but also a willingness to confront the shadows that lurked beneath the surface.

As she watched the girl's retreating figure disappear into the distance, Nikki knew that her own healing journey had taken an unexpected turn. The encounters she had witnessed, the fragmented stories that wove themselves into her consciousness—they all demanded her attention, urging her to step out of the bubble of grief and into the embrace of a world that yearned for redemption and renewal.

And so, with a newfound resolve, Nikki embraced the uncertain road that lay ahead.

She would no longer be a passive observer but an active participant, weaving her own story into the intricate fabric of life. For it was in the shared struggles, the intertwining narratives, that true healing could be found.

Nikki had taken refuge in the quiet solace of the gym, seeking solace in the rhythmic movement of her body on the treadmill. The steady thump of her footsteps provided a temporary respite from the relentless thoughts that plagued her mind. As she focused on the distant horizon, her heart heavy with the weight of grief and longing, a familiar figure caught her attention.

On the adjacent treadmill, the woman she had witnessed in the midst of a heated argument just days ago now worked her body with determined intensity. The memory of their encounter lingered in Nikki's mind, a fragment of a story she was both curious and apprehensive to explore. But for now, they remained silent companions, their unspoken connection echoing within the walls of the gym.

As Nikki continued her workout, her mind wandered through the realms of possibility. She yearned for the comfort of her old life, the familiar embrace of George's presence. It was a longing she couldn't deny, even as the desire for a fresh start tugged at the fringes of her consciousness. The dichotomy between holding onto the past and embracing the unknown pulled at her heartstrings, leaving her torn between two opposing forces.

The minutes ticked by the rhythmic hum of exercise machines filling the air. Megan, the woman Nikki had observed, finished her workout, and gathered her belongings. A fleeting glance passed between them, a silent acknowledgment of their shared experience. But before Nikki could gather the courage to break the silence, Megan swiftly departed, leaving Nikki alone with her thoughts.

As Nikki stepped off the treadmill, a sense of unease prickled at the back of her neck. The gym, once a sanctuary from the outside world, now seemed suffused with an air of foreboding. She couldn't shake the feeling that she was being watched, that unseen eyes trailed her every move.

Determined to dismiss her growing paranoia, Nikki gathered her belongings and headed for the exit. The warm air of the outside world greeted her, offering a temporary reprieve from the confines of the gym. Yet, as she stepped onto the sidewalk, her senses sharpened, attuned to the slightest sound or movement.

A shiver ran down her spine as a fleeting figure caught the corner of her eye—a silhouette lingering in the periphery of her vision. Instinctively, she quickened her pace, her footsteps echoing with a mix of apprehension and curiosity. The sensation of being followed clung to her like a shadow, growing with each passing moment.

She dared not turn her head, fearing that her actions would only confirm her suspicions. Instead, Nikki focused on her surroundings, scanning the streets and the faces of those passing by. The bustling city unfolded before her; its vibrant energy interwoven with the underlying tension that gripped her heart.

A strange mixture of fear and determination welled within her. Whoever was following her, whatever secrets lay hidden in the depths of their intentions, she refused to be a passive observer once again. The echoes of George's memory spurred her forward, igniting a flicker of courage that burned brightly within her.

Nikki sat in the solitude of her living room, the dim glow of the lamp casting a soft illumination on the surrounding space. It was another sleepless night, the familiar torment of insomnia persisting since the day George passed away. The weight of grief settled heavily upon her, intertwining with the haunting visions that plagued her restless mind.

She closed her eyes, trying to shut out the memories that lingered just beyond her grasp. Yet, when she least expected it, the image of George would materialize, his presence so vivid it felt as if he stood before her. In those moments, the boundaries between reality and illusion blurred, granting her a fleeting respite from the crushing loneliness that enveloped her existence.

The visions of George were both a blessing and a curse, a bittersweet reminder of the love they had shared and the dreams they had cherished. They offered solace in the depths of her sorrow, a glimpse of the life they were meant to live together—a life of adventure and exploration across Western Europe.

As Nikki's mind wandered through the corridors of memory, she pondered her sister's suggestion of therapy. The notion of seeking professional help had lingered at the back of her mind, an ever-present whisper urging her towards healing and understanding. But the fear of losing the hallucinations of George held her back, a fragile thread connecting her to the world they once shared.

Therapy, she believed, would unravel the tapestry of her grief, laying bare the painful truths she had yet to confront. It would be a necessary step towards healing, towards reclaiming her own identity outside the realm of her lost love. But the thought of bidding farewell to the spectral presence that haunted her waking hours was almost unbearable.

She was not yet ready to relinquish the tender moments she shared with George, even if they existed solely within the realms of her mind. The visions provided solace, a fragile bridge between past and present, and she clung to them as if they were lifelines keeping her afloat amidst the turbulent seas of her grief.

Nikki knew that therapy held the promise of uncovering buried emotions, of dissecting the complex tapestry of her loss. It offered the opportunity to confront her pain head-on, to navigate the jagged fragments of her shattered heart. But the fear of relinquishing the hallucinations of George, of severing the ethereal connection they shared, paralyzed her in her quest for healing.

She recognized that one day she would have to face the inevitability of letting go, of embracing a future that lay beyond the reach of her departed love. But for now, she clung to the visions, finding solace in the flicker of familiarity they brought to her turbulent nights.

CHAPTER FIVE.

The solitude of her home had become both a sanctuary and a prison for Nikki in the wake of George's passing. Days turned into weeks, and weeks blurred into months, as she found solace in the familiar routines of her occasional outings. On this particular Tuesday evening, a restless energy surged through her veins, compelling her to step out into the world beyond her door.

As Nikki ventured out into the cool night, she felt a tingling anticipation prickling at the back of her neck. The city streets were illuminated by the soft glow of streetlights, casting long shadows that danced to the rhythm of passing cars. Seeking a change of scenery, she found herself drawn towards the underpass, where the rumbling engines reverberated through the concrete pillars.

Standing beneath the underpass, Nikki leaned against the cold wall, the vibrations of passing vehicles resonating through her body. The steady hum and the rush of wind stirred her senses, momentarily distracting her from the weight of her grief. She gazed into the distance, feeling the weight of the world pressing down on her shoulders.

As she resumed her journey home, a sense of unease settled over Nikki. She quickened her pace, her footsteps echoing against the silent streets. It was then that she noticed a figure emerging from the shadows, clad in a nondescript hooded sweatshirt that concealed their features. A shiver ran down her spine as she felt their gaze fixated upon her, even though their faces remained hidden in darkness.

Nikki's instincts screamed at her to cross the street, to avoid any potential danger that this mysterious figure might pose. Yet, an inexplicable curiosity rooted her feet to the ground. She couldn't tear her eyes away, compelled by an unspoken connection that seemed to defy reason.

The man in the hooded sweatshirt continued to advance, his steps deliberate and purposeful. Every fiber of Nikki's being screamed at her to flee, to seek safety within the confines of her home. But something, perhaps a remnant of the adventurous spirit she had shared with George, urged her to confront the unknown.

Their paths intersected, and for a brief moment, their eyes locked. Nikki strained to see through the shadowy hood, searching for any sign, any glimpse of recognition. But the man remained an enigma, a phantom haunting the periphery of her consciousness.

A shudder coursed through her as the hooded figure passed by, his presence leaving an indelible imprint on her senses. It was as if the air had thickened, a palpable tension clinging to her skin. Nikki's heart pounded in her chest, a mix of fear and curiosity intertwining within her.

Nikki stood in her dimly lit kitchen, the weight of grief heavy upon her shoulders. The allure of the wine bottle beckoned to her, promising a temporary respite from the ache that consumed her. She knew deep down that drowning her sorrows in alcohol would only provide fleeting relief if any at all. But at that moment, the numbness seemed preferable to the raw, unyielding pain.

As she reached for the bottle, her hand trembling, a familiar presence manifested before her eyes. George, her beloved late husband, materialized as a vision, his warm smile a balm to her wounded soul. He shook his head gently as if urging her to reconsider.

In that fleeting moment of connection, Nikki understood the message conveyed by George's ghostly presence. He had always been her rock, her voice of reason, even in the face of his own struggles. His mere presence reminded her of the strength they had shared, the resilience that had carried them through the darkest of times.

With a heavy sigh, Nikki withdrew her hand from the bottle. She knew deep within herself that succumbing to the numbing embrace of alcohol would not bring her solace, but rather prolong her journey toward healing. George's smile held a silent promise, a reminder that she could find strength within herself.

Resolutely, Nikki walked over to the sink and poured the crimson liquid down the drain. The sound of the wine splashing against the porcelain was a symbolic release—a shedding of the temporary escape and an embrace of the pain that needed to be felt, processed, and eventually healed.

In the quiet solitude of her bedroom, Nikki slipped beneath the covers, her mind still reeling from the encounter with George's vision. Although the pain of his absence remained, a spark of determination flickered within her. She knew that seeking refuge in unhealthy coping mechanisms would only prolong her journey toward acceptance and inner peace.

Nikki's eyes shot open; her body instantly tense as she was pulled from the depths of slumber. The soft glow of moonlight bathed her bedroom, casting eerie shadows on the walls. It was 3 a.m., the hour when darkness and silence enveloped the world, leaving room for the unknown to tiptoe into the corners of her mind.

A familiar sense of unease washed over her as she registered the sound of persistent knocking, echoing through the stillness of her home. Her heart thudded in her chest, matching the rhythm of the unsettling disturbance that had shattered her sleep.

Unwilling to ignore the source of the disturbance, Nikki threw off her blankets and swung her legs over the edge of the bed. Her bare feet met the cool hardwood floor, sending a shiver up her spine. With every step, the anticipation grew, mingling with a cocktail of fear and curiosity.

As she made her way across the landing, her mind raced with a multitude of questions. Who could be standing on her doorstep at this hour? What could possibly warrant such urgency? The baseball bat that leaned against the wall caught her eye, and without hesitation, she snatched it up, finding some semblance of reassurance in its familiar weight.

Down the stairs she went, each creaking step a reminder of the unnerving situation that awaited her. The darkened hallway stretched out before her, its shadows morphing into phantoms dancing at the periphery of her vision. Her grip tightened around the bat as she approached the front door.

And as the door swung open, revealing the truth that lay concealed in the shadows, Nikki braced herself for whatever awaited her, the haunting echoes of George's warning fading into the recesses of her memory.

Standing on the other side of the door was the same tall, dark stranger she had seen at the harbor, and again on the subway. The haunting familiarity sent a shiver down Nikki's spine, her senses heightened with unease. How had he found her? It seemed he had followed her home, an unwelcome presence invading her sanctuary. He peered at her with quizzical eyes, an unsettling gaze that hinted at hidden depths.

Then, he uttered a question that pierced through the fragile boundaries of her world.

"Is this where my dad lived?"

Nikki knew without a doubt that the stranger was mistaken. Her heart pounded, and she desperately sought refuge in the realm of reason, trying to make sense of the inexplicable. Yet, the man's peculiar behavior struck her with unease. Every few seconds, a surge of paranoia seemed to overcome him, compelling him to cup his chin with a hand that rubbed incessantly at his face. His skin had grown flushed from the repeated scratching, leaving visible traces of agitation. But it didn't stop there. His hand would abruptly drop, and his body would recoil with a faint, hollow thud against his sternum. The sequence of movements appeared involuntary as if he were locked in a disquieting battle with himself. It was an uncomfortable spectacle to witness, an unraveling of sanity that left Nikki on edge. At times, he seemed barely lucid, trapped within the confines of his own mind.

He resembled one of those desperate souls you instinctively veer away from on the street, the kind who strives to catch your gaze before igniting an odd conversation. There was a sense of fragmentation about him as if he were pieced together from shards of shattered humanity.

"You cool?" the burning-eyed man muttered, his hand instinctively returning to touch his face once again.

Nikki's throat tightened, and she cleared it nervously, her body poised for an impending lunge that felt all too possible. "I'm Nikki," she managed to say, her voice tinged with caution. "I'm sorry, but it's just me here. Now, please..."

"But not always, right?" the man interrupted, tugging at his sleeve with a twitch of desperation.

Confusion clouded Nikki's expression as she furrowed her brow, trying to decipher his cryptic words. "What are you talking about?" she asked, her voice tinged with rising irritation. "I don't know who you are, but you have the wrong house. Now, please leave."

A shadow fell across the man's face, bitterness seeping into his voice. "You really don't know who I am, do you?" he retorted, his words laced with an undercurrent of wounded pride. "My name is Junior... George Junior. George Lewis was my father."

CHAPTER SIX.

Nikki's mind raced, tangled in a web of conflicting emotions. The revelation that George, her late husband, had a son felt like a betrayal of their shared existence. They had been partners, confidants who held nothing back from each other. How could he have kept such a significant secret hidden from her? Doubt clawed at her, mingling with the grief and anger that surged within her veins. It couldn't be true. George would never do this to her.

Yet, a subtle twinge of curiosity seeped through the cracks in her disbelief. The words that Junior had uttered lingered, like a haunting melody she couldn't escape. Could it be true? Nikki desperately wished for it to be lies, a fabrication born out of malice or deceit. Perhaps it was some kind of elaborate scam, an attempt to disrupt the delicate balance of her existence.

"How do I know you're telling the truth?" Nikki's voice trembled with uncertainty, her eyes fixed on Junior, searching for any hint of deception.

Junior sighed, a weariness settling upon him as he reached for his wallet. With deliberate movements, he retrieved a photograph and held it out for Nikki to see. It depicted him standing alongside a woman who exuded warmth and a man who bore an undeniable resemblance to George. Nikki's breath caught in her throat as she studied the image, the weight of the revelation crashing down upon her.

"That's my dad," Junior pointed to the man in the photograph, his voice tinged with a mixture of sadness and longing. "I have more pictures and documents at home if you want to see them."

Nikki's gaze remained locked on the photograph, her mind a maelstrom of emotions. The resemblance between Junior and George was undeniable, a painful reminder of the secrets that had been woven into the fabric of their lives. Grief and anger churned within her, directed both at George for his deception and at herself for not uncovering the truth earlier.

"Look, I don't know what to say," Nikki finally spoke, her voice laden with the weight of her shattered reality. "I can't... I can't believe this. No! My husband would've told me."

Understanding flickered in Junior's eyes as he nodded softly, his voice a gentle plea. "I understand," he said, his words carrying the weight of shared sorrow. "But please, don't push me away. I just want to know my dad and connect with his family."

Nikki stood there, her heart torn between the desire to protect the memories of her husband and the lingering curiosity sparked by Junior's presence. The room brimmed with unspoken truths, the fragile connection between them teetering on the precipice of acceptance or denial. At that moment, Nikki found herself grappling with the ghosts of her past, unsure of the path that lay ahead.

Nikki stood frozen on her front doorstep, her hand clutching the baseball bat tightly. She couldn't believe what she had just heard from the stranger, Junior. He had just revealed that he was the secret son of her late husband, George. It was impossible, or at least that's what she told herself.

"What are you saying?" Nikki asked, her voice shaking. "That's not possible. You're lying. George would never keep something like that from me."

Junior tried to reason with her, to explain that he had only recently learned the truth himself, but Nikki was too shocked to listen. She refused to believe what he was saying, and her mind was racing with questions and doubts.

"Please, Nikki," Junior pleaded, taking a step closer to her. "I know this is a shock, but it's the truth. I can prove it to you. Just give me a chance."

Nikki's grip on the bat tightened, and she took a step back, interpreting his approach as a sign of aggression.

"Stay away from me," she warned, her voice rising in panic. "I don't know who you are, or what you want, but you need to leave. Now."

Junior's face fell, and he backed away from her, his hands raised in surrender.

"I'm not here to hurt you, Nikki," he said, his voice low and pleading. "I just want to talk to you, to tell you about my father, your husband. Please, just give me a chance."

Nikki hesitated for a moment, her mind racing with conflicting emotions. She wanted to believe Junior, but her grief and anger were clouding her judgment. She raised the bat, ready to swing again, when Junior made a sudden move towards her.

In a split second, Nikki swung the bat with all her might, connecting with Junior's head. He looked at her for a moment, his eyes wide with shock, and then collapsed on the ground.

Nikki dropped the bat, horrified by what she had done. She ran to Junior's side, but it was too late. He was unconscious, and blood was pooling around his head.

Nikki stood frozen by the body; her eyes fixed on Junior's lifeless form. Blood pooled around him, staining the ground like a crimson canvas. The bat slipped from her trembling hand, falling to the ground. A cold shiver coursed through her, and she felt a weight settle on her shoulders.

In that moment, time seemed to stand still, and Nikki's mind became a swirling vortex of memories and emotions. And then, as if conjured by her thoughts, a vision of George materialized before her. He stood there, a silent observer, his eyes penetrating her soul. His presence was both comforting and unsettling, like a ghostly echo from the past.

Nikki's heart ached with a mix of longing, guilt, and confusion. She had loved George deeply, and their bond had been unbreakable. But now, faced with the revelation of Junior's existence, she couldn't help but question everything she thought she knew about her husband.

George's gaze held a depth of understanding as if he knew the turmoil raging within her. His silence spoke volumes, and it was in that silence that Nikki found herself searching for answers. Why had he kept Junior a secret? What other truths had he concealed from her?

The weight on Nikki's shoulders grew heavier, and she felt the weight of her own actions. She wished she could turn back time, undo her impulsive act, and find a way to reconcile the conflicting emotions that threatened to consume her.

Nikki's mind was clouded with panic as she dragged the body into the house and closed the door behind her. The weight of the situation bore down on her, suffocating her thoughts. She had to think, to make a decision. Should she call the police? Should she hide the truth? The answers eluded her, slipping through her fingers like smoke.

As she stood there, her gaze fixed on the lifeless form before her, her mind wandered to George and the revelation of his secret life. Another family. How could he have kept such a significant part of himself hidden from her? The pain of betrayal welled up within her, intertwining with the fear and confusion that gripped her.

Her eyes darted around the room, searching for answers, for any clues that could help her make sense of this nightmare. Her thoughts flitted to the note she had found, the one that hinted at secrets untold. And then there was the photograph, capturing a moment frozen in time, a glimpse into a world she had never known existed.

With a sudden surge of determination, Nikki made up her mind. She needed to understand, to uncover the truth that had been concealed from her. Her thoughts drifted to George's office, a place she hadn't entered since his death. Perhaps there, amidst the remnants of his life's work, she would find the missing pieces of the puzzle.

The weight of the body seemed to seep into the very fabric of the house, a constant reminder of the choices she had made. She knew she couldn't hide forever, that the truth would inevitably catch up to her. But for now, she needed time, time to gather her thoughts, to confront the web of secrets that had entangled her existence.

Nikki stood at the threshold of George's office, her hand hesitating on the doorknob. It had been a year since she last set foot in this room, and a surge of unease washed over her. Memories, both bitter and sweet, tugged at her heart, reminding her of a life that had been abruptly severed.

With a deep breath, Nikki pushed open the door and stepped inside. The room lay before her like a time capsule, frozen in a state of suspended animation. The air was thick with dust, each particle seemingly holding a fragment of their shared past. The sunlight filtered through the half-drawn blinds, casting elongated shadows that danced upon the worn carpet.

Her eyes roamed the space, taking in the remnants of a life once lived. The desk, cluttered with papers, bore witness to the untold stories that had unfolded within these walls. A half-empty coffee mug stood sentinel; its contents long gone cold. The bookshelves sagged under the weight of countless volumes, their spines cracked and well-worn, a testament to George's insatiable thirst for knowledge.

Nikki moved cautiously; her footsteps muffled by the silence that enveloped the room. She ran her fingers along the edge of the desk, tracing the grooves left by years of use. A pang of longing surged through her, an ache for the familiar rhythm of their intertwined lives.

As she ventured deeper into the room, Nikki's gaze fell upon the photographs adorning the walls. Frozen smiles stared back at her, moments captured in time that now seemed distant and elusive. She wondered about the stories behind those faces, the lives that had intersected with George's in ways she could never fully comprehend.

A drawer caught her attention, slightly ajar as if tempting her to delve into its secrets.

With a mix of curiosity and trepidation, Nikki pulled it open, revealing a trove of memories. Letters, faded and yellowed with age, lay nestled among forgotten trinkets and mementos. Each item whispered a tale of love, loss, and hidden desires.

PART TWO - BATTLING WITH THE TRUTH

CHAPTER SEVEN.

My Dearest Nikki,

I hope this letter finds you in good health and spirits. I write these words with a heavy heart, burdened by the weight of a truth that I should have shared with you long ago. It is a truth that has haunted me, silently weaving its way through the tapestry of our lives, leaving behind a threadbare fabric of secrets and regrets.

Years before our paths crossed, I had a son with another woman. A son who bore witness to my shortcomings as a father, my inability to provide the love and stability that every child deserves. For reasons I cannot fully comprehend myself, I drifted in and out of his life, an absent presence whose intermittent presence only added to the confusion and pain.

I cannot excuse my actions, nor can I expect forgiveness for the wounds I have inflicted upon you by keeping this truth hidden. I chose silence, driven by fear and a misplaced sense of protection. But in doing so, I denied you the opportunity to understand the complexities of my past, and the struggles I faced in reconciling my responsibilities as a father with the love I found in you.

Nikki, you must know that you were the catalyst for change in my life. In your presence, I found solace and the strength to confront my shortcomings, to strive towards becoming the man I longed to be. Your unwavering love and unwavering belief in me compelled me to examine my past actions, to seek redemption for the mistakes I had made.

I am deeply sorry for the pain and confusion that my silence has caused you. I should have shared this burden with you, allowing us to navigate the complexities of our lives together. I should have trusted in your understanding, in the capacity of your heart to embrace the flaws of our shared humanity.

If you are reading this letter, it means that circumstances have prevented me from bidding you a proper farewell. I can only hope that my words will serve as a testament to the love I hold for you, a love that has shaped me, transformed me, and given me the strength to confront my past and strive toward a better future.

Nikki, you made me a better man. Your presence in my life taught me the true meaning of love, of sacrifice, and of forgiveness. Though I faltered in my responsibilities as a father, I promise you that I will never stop loving you. I never stopped cherishing the moments we shared, the laughter, the tears, and the unspoken understanding that bound us together.

I implore you to find it in your heart to forgive me, to release the burdens of resentment that I have imposed upon you. Know that my intentions were never malicious but born out of fear and flawed judgment. You deserve the truth, the whole truth, and I am truly sorry for denying you that.

If there is one thing, I hope you take from this letter, it is the knowledge that my love for you knows no bounds. In life or death, my heart will forever beat for you, whispering words of gratitude for the love you bestowed upon me and prayers for your happiness and peace.

Please, remember me not for the flaws and mistakes I have made, but for the love that flowed between us. For the moments of joy, of understanding, and of connection that made our time together so precious. And most importantly, remember that you were my anchor, my guiding light, and the force that drove me to be a better man.

With all the love that resides within me, George

My Son,

If you are reading this letter, it means that circumstances have prevented us from crossing paths in person, that our lives have followed divergent paths without the opportunity for me to witness your growth and be the father you deserved. It is with a heavy heart and the weight of regret that I pen these words, hoping that somehow, they will find their way to you and provide some semblance of closure.

I want you to know that I am your father. From the moment you took your first breath, a bond was formed between us that transcends time and distance. Despite my absence, my thoughts and love have always been with you, even if they have remained unspoken and hidden.

Life has a way of twisting and turning, of throwing obstacles in our path that we never anticipated. There were circumstances beyond my control that kept us apart, that prevented me from being the father you needed and deserved. For that, I am truly sorry.

I cannot offer excuses or justifications for my absence, for the moments I missed and the void I left in your life. All I can do is express my deepest remorse and hope that you will find it in your heart to forgive me, to understand that my intentions were never to abandon you but were born out of circumstances beyond my control.

As you navigate your own journey through life, I implore you to be better, to do better than I did. Learn from my mistakes and choose a path that is defined by honesty, integrity, and love. Embrace the opportunities that come your way, cherish the connections you form, and never shy away from expressing your emotions and showing those you care about how much they mean to you.

Remember, my son, that life is unpredictable, and the road ahead may be filled with challenges and hardships. But it is in those moments that your character will be tested, that you will have the chance to rise above and leave a positive mark on the world. Choose kindness over cruelty, empathy over indifference, and always strive to be the best version of yourself.

I write this letter with a heavy heart, knowing — *THE LETTER REMAINED UNFINISHED.*

*

Diary Entry: Several Months After Marrying Nikki

September 12th

It has been several months since Nikki and I exchanged our vows, promising to build a life together filled with love and trust. Our days have been filled with laughter and joy, and I cherish every moment we spend together. But today, a specter from the past emerged, shattering the fragile peace we had managed to create.

Mama, my mother, showed up unannounced at our doorstep, her weary eyes filled with longing. I haven't seen her in years, ever since I left home to pursue a life separate from the chaos that consumed us. Her presence, both comforting and unsettling, brings back memories that I had hoped to keep buried.

She pleaded with me, her voice trembling, begging for us to be a family once more. Her vulnerability tore at my heart, and for a moment, I considered granting her request. But I couldn't ignore the consequences it would bring. Nikki, the woman I love with all my heart, deserves to be shielded from the pain that follows in my wake. I cannot risk exposing her to the turbulence of my past, the secrets I carry. The choice I made, to protect Nikki and keep our home a sanctuary, weighs heavily upon me.

Diary Entry: The Burden of Secrets

January 6th

The weight of my secret is becoming unbearable, threatening to consume me from within. How can I keep such a significant part of my life hidden from Nikki, the person who shares my bed and my dreams? Each day, I see her radiant smile and the trust shining in her eyes, and it pierces my soul with guilt.

But how can I unravel the tangled web of lies without destroying everything we've built? I fear losing her, losing us. Yet, the truth gnaws at me relentlessly, reminding me that true intimacy cannot be built on a foundation of deception. It's a cruel paradox, torn between protecting Nikki from the pain of my past and longing for the freedom that truth brings.

I know I can no longer bear this burden alone. I must find a way to confess, to reveal the darkest corners of my heart, and hope that Nikki will understand, that she will still love me once she sees the scars I carry.

April 30th

Today, I watched Nikki as she wept silently, her eyes filled with anguish and desperation. The doctor's words echoed in our ears, piercing through the fragile bubble of hope we had clung to for so long. Infertility, they said, a cruel blow that shattered our dreams of starting a family together.

My heart ached, torn between the guilt of harboring a secret and the pain of our shared loss. How could I grieve the inability to conceive when I already have a child of my own out there, a child who does not know of my existence? The weight of that guilt threatens to drown me, suffocating my very being.

Nikki, unaware of the truth that haunts me, clings to my hand, seeking solace in our shared pain. In her eyes, I see the flicker of hope dimming, replaced by an overwhelming sadness that pierces my soul. How can I find the courage to tell her the truth, to expose the wounds that have festered in silence?

I pray for guidance, for a path that will lead us out of this darkness. I yearn for forgiveness, from Nikki and from myself, and the strength to confront the tangled threads of our lives.

July 18th

Today, I ventured into the realm of the past, hoping to rekindle the flickering embers of a lost connection. I met with my parents, the same ones who abandoned me, at a cozy little coffee shop near our home. It had been years since we last saw each other, and I had carried a glimmer of hope that we could rebuild what was shattered long ago.

But hope turned to disappointment as the conversation unfolded. They were distant, guarded, and unwilling to let me back into their lives. They refused to offer any explanation for their absence, for the void they left in my heart. I sensed their discomfort, their reluctance to delve into the wounds of the past. And though they remained silent, I had my suspicions, the pieces of a painful puzzle falling into place.

My heart aches, the rejection casting a shadow over my fragile sense of self. But I cannot force them to confront their demons, nor can I hold on to a dream that was never meant to be. I must accept their choice and find solace in the family I have built with Nikki, in the love that binds us together.

September 3rd

Dark clouds gather in the corners of my mind, accompanied by persistent headaches that plague me day and night. The pain cuts through my thoughts, leaving me disoriented and fatigued. Something is amiss, and I can no longer ignore the whispers of concern that creep into my consciousness.

Tomorrow, I will visit the doctor, hoping for answers that will dispel this unsettling uncertainty. But in the depths of my soul, I cannot shake the fear that lingers, the fear that this pain holds a deeper meaning, a foreboding message that I dare not utter aloud.

Nikki, my love, my pillar of strength, I cannot help but feel torn. If anything were to happen to me, if these shadows that haunt me prove to be more than passing clouds, I want you to know the truth. The truth about my hidden past, about the secrets that have weighed upon my soul. You deserve to know, before it's too late, before the curtain falls and the opportunity for reconciliation slips through our fingers.

November 10th

The doctor's diagnosis was both a relief and a source of concern. Migraines, they said, are the cause of my persistent headaches and the ever-present haze that clouds my vision. While I am grateful that it is nothing more sinister, the underlying unease remains. They said if it continues, they can put me through more tests.

As the pain ebbs and flows, I find myself reflecting on the choices I have made, on the secrets I have guarded so fiercely. I am filled with an overwhelming urge to unburden myself, to share the weight that has become too heavy to bear alone. If these migraines persist, if they become something more, I fear the truth will be lost forever, swallowed by the void of my unspoken words.

CHAPTER EIGHT.

Nikki's mind reeled with disbelief, her eyes fixated on the photographs and letters that lay on the desk before her. The images captured a world she had never known, a secret woven into the very fabric of her husband's existence. A woman, radiant and smiling, stood beside two innocent children, their eyes sparkling with unbridled joy. They were a family, a second family, hidden away from Nikki's gaze.

Tears cascaded down Nikki's cheeks, tracing a path of heartbreak as her shattered illusions fell into sharp focus. The man she had loved, the man she had built a life with, had harbored a clandestine world, concealed beneath layers of deceit. The weight of betrayal settled heavily upon her shoulders, threatening to crush her spirit.

Amidst the anguish, a surge of realization coursed through Nikki's veins. She had left the stranger's lifeless body unattended in the hallway, consumed by the tumult of her discovery. Panic gripped her as she hurriedly retraced her steps, her feet echoing against the walls, each stride carrying the weight of uncertainty.

But when she arrived at the spot where the body had fallen, an unsettling emptiness greeted her. It was as though the stranger had evaporated into thin air, leaving behind only the lingering echoes of their violent encounter. Nikki's pulse quickened, her breath growing shallow as she scanned the surroundings, searching for any trace of the man's presence.

Fear danced upon the edges of her consciousness, whispering cruel doubts into her ears. Had he managed to escape, slipping away with the remnants of her secrets? Was he lurking in the shadows, his presence a menacing specter haunting the confines of her home? The uncertainty gnawed at her sanity, turning her sanctuary into a chamber of paranoia.

Nikki's mind raced, desperately seeking an anchor amidst the tempest of her thoughts. Should she call the authorities? Should she confess the truth, lay bare the tangle of her own secrets? Confusion clouded her judgment, leaving her stranded in a murky sea of indecision.

The weight of her actions bore down upon her, an unrelenting burden that threatened to suffocate her. She had acted in self-defense, an instinctual response to the threat before her. But now, the consequences of her choices loomed large, casting shadows of doubt upon her conscience.

As the minutes slipped away, Nikki stood at the precipice of a choice that would define her future. She could embrace the darkness that beckoned, allow herself to be consumed by fear and guilt. Or she could summon the strength within, confront the truth that lay dormant within her, and face the consequences head-on.

With a flicker of determination igniting within her, Nikki took a deep breath, the resolve hardening in her gaze. The storm of uncertainty would not claim her. She would navigate the treacherous waters, guided by the beacon of truth, as she braced herself for the revelations and repercussions that lay in wait.

Nikki's hands trembled as she scrubbed away the traces of blood staining the cold, unforgiving floor. The sight of it made her stomach churn, a grim reminder of the violence that had unfolded within the confines of her home. The body was gone now, disappeared into the night, leaving behind a trail of unanswered questions that gnawed at Nikki's mind.

Thoughts raced in chaotic patterns, intertwining, and colliding like frenzied dancers on an unlit stage. Had he managed to escape, slipping away in the darkness, leaving Nikki alone to grapple with the aftermath of their violent encounter? Or had someone intervened, whisking him away to conceal the truth of that fateful night? The uncertainty weighed heavily upon her, suffocating her with its relentless grip.

She had never intended to hurt anyone, not truly. It had been an act of self-defense, an instinctual response borne out of desperation and fear. Yet, in the silence that now enveloped her home, doubts gnawed at her conscience. Had she gone too far? Was there another way to have protected herself without resorting to violence?

Restlessness consumed Nikki, twisting, and turning within her like a taut wire, its sharp edges piercing her thoughts. Sleep eluded her, slipping through her grasp like fine sand through the gaps of her fingers. The adrenaline that had coursed through her veins during that fateful encounter refused to subside, leaving her wired and on edge.

Seeking solace, she curled up on the worn couch, her body sinking into the familiar embrace of the cushions. The world outside lay shrouded in darkness, the night casting its own brand of secrets and uncertainties. The rhythmic ticking of the clock echoed through the silent room, a metronome of her restless thoughts.

As Nikki waited, her mind played host to a myriad of possibilities. Would the dawn bring relief or further complications? Would the truth be revealed, or would it forever remain hidden in the shadows? The weight of anticipation pressed upon her chest, the heaviness of uncertainty carving deep furrows upon her brow.

In the stillness of the night, she sought refuge in solitude, allowing her thoughts to wander down labyrinthine paths. What had led her to this point? How had her life taken such a harrowing turn? The ghosts of her choices danced within the recesses of her mind, their spectral fingers brushing against the edges of her consciousness.

Dawn approached with cautious footsteps, a glimmer of pale light piercing through the curtains, as if offering a timid glimpse into the realm of possibilities. Nikki remained curled on the couch, her body taut with anticipation, her mind entangled in a web of hope and trepidation.

Morning would bring its own revelations, its own set of consequences. The world would awaken, unaware of the turmoil that had unfolded within the confines of Nikki's home. The hours ahead held the power to reshape her destiny, to steer her path toward redemption or despair.

With each passing second, Nikki's restless soul clung to a fragile thread of hope, yearning for the clarity that awaited her as the first rays of sunlight pierced through the veil of night. And so, she braced herself, her heart filled with a strange mix of dread and anticipation, as the hours ticked away, counting down to the arrival of morning's revelation.

Nikki tosses and turns in her sleep, her mind plagued by nightmares. She is back in the dark room with Mama and Junior, her abductors. They are taunting her, telling her that they will never let her go. She tries to scream, but no sound comes out of her mouth. The room starts to spin, and Nikki feels like she's about to be sick. Suddenly, she wakes up, her heart pounding in her chest.

Nikki woke up to the sound of birds chirping outside her window. She felt exhausted and drained after the emotional turmoil of the previous day. Her mind was a blur of memories and revelations, and she wasn't sure how to process it all.

She lay in bed, staring at the ceiling, lost in thought, trying to make sense of everything she had learned about her late husband George's secret family. The more she thought about it, the angrier she became. How could George have kept something so significant from her for all these years? How could he have a whole other family and not even tell her about it?

As she lay there, she could feel the weight of the betrayal and the hurt crushing down on her. She tried to push it away, but it was all-consuming.

Nikki's phone buzzed, and she saw a message from her sister Kayla asking how she was doing. She didn't even know how to begin to answer that question.

She got up and walked to the bathroom, staring at herself in the mirror. Her eyes were red and puffy from crying, and she looked like she hadn't slept in days.

Nikki splashed cold water on her face, hoping it would help her snap out of the fog she was in. But the pain and the confusion were still there, gnawing at her.

She took a deep breath and decided that she couldn't let herself be consumed by this pain. She needed to figure out a way to move forward, to find a way to make sense of everything that had happened.

THIRTY-THREE.

Nikki jolted awake, gasping for breath, her body drenched in perspiration. Beads of sweat trickled down her forehead as the remnants of a haunting dream clung to her senses, refusing to dissipate. It was a nightmare that had woven itself into the fabric of her subconscious, leaving her trembling with a mixture of fear and confusion.

As Nikki tried to steady her racing heart, a memory of George, her ex-boyfriend, surfaced in her mind. It was a memory that held a tinge of sadness, one that had been buried deep within the recesses of her thoughts. Around three years ago, when they were still together, Nikki had brought George a sandwich while he was working in his cluttered office. The memory was vivid, like a snapshot frozen in time.

She remembered the hesitant smile that graced her lips as she approached his desk, hoping to surprise him and bring a moment of respite to his busy day. But the atmosphere shifted the moment he laid eyes on the sandwich. His expression hardened, his eyes narrowing with an unexplainable intensity. Confusion etched itself onto Nikki's face as she searched for answers in the depths of his reaction.

However, she found none. Instead, George's reaction had been defensive and abrupt, as if the simple act of kindness had triggered a hidden storm within him. He had snapped at her, his voice laced with anger and frustration, leaving Nikki stunned and hurt. In that moment, she had questioned herself, wondering what she had done wrong, what unspoken pain lay behind his outburst.

George had been hiding a secret life from her, and she couldn't help but wonder how many other things he had kept hidden from her.

Nikki closed her eyes and tried to focus on the good memories of George. She remembered the way he would laugh at her jokes, the sound of his voice, and the way he would hold her when she was feeling sad.

But the memory kept nagging at her, and she couldn't shake the feeling that there was more to the story.

As she sipped her coffee, she closed her eyes and tried to remember the details of that day. She could picture George sitting at his desk, typing away on his computer. She could see the way his brow furrowed as he focused on his work.

And then she remembered how he had reacted when she brought him the sandwich. He had snapped at her, accusing her of trying to distract him from his work. She had been hurt by his reaction but had brushed it off as just a bad day.

Now, though, she knew that it was more than that. George had been hiding a secret life, and her intrusion had been a threat to that secret.

CHAPTER NINE.

N ikki sat on the couch, her thoughts consumed by the bittersweet memories of George and the life they had once shared. Lost in the realm of nostalgia, she wandered through the corridors of their history together, each memory a shard of joy and pain. But her reverie shattered when she looked up and saw him standing in the doorway of the living room.

Her heart wrenched with a potent mix of longing and sorrow. George, the man she had loved deeply, now stood before her, a figure both familiar and estranged. A surge of conflicting emotions threatened to engulf her, pulling her in opposite directions. One part of her yearned to run into his arms, to seek solace in his embrace. Yet, another part, wounded and resentful, demanded distance and self-preservation.

Nikki blinked away tears as her voice emerged in a whisper, trembling with a raw vulnerability. "Go," she implored, her words laced with a palpable ache.

George's features shifted from sadness to confusion, his eyes searching for understanding. "Please, baby..." he began, his voice laced with remorse.

"I said go," Nikki reiterated, her voice growing stronger, resolute. "I don't want to see you right now."

With each syllable, a wave of anguish washed over her, mingling with the remnants of their shattered connection. The wounds were still raw, the pain etched into her very being. She needed distance, a respite from the tumultuous emotions that threatened to engulf her.

George took a hesitant step forward, his hand extended in a gesture of pleading. "Nikki, please," he implored, his voice tinged with desperation. "Let me explain. I never meant to hurt you."

Tears streamed down Nikki's face, mingling with the anguish etched upon her features. She shook her head, a mixture of sorrow and determination coursing through her veins. "I can't do this right now," she confessed, her voice laden with a heavy sigh. "I need time to process everything, to untangle the web of emotions that entwines our past. Please, just go."

The plea held both a plea and a demand—a plea for respite, for a moment of respite from the storm that raged within her, and a demand for the space she needed to heal. She knew that confronting the complexities of their relationship, of the pain that had etched itself into her heart, required a sanctuary of solitude.

George's eyes flickered with a mix of remorse and understanding, his outstretched hand retreating slowly. He nodded, a silent acknowledgment of the pain he had caused. "I understand," he whispered, his voice heavy with regret. "I'll give you the time you need."

With those words, George turned on his heel and left, his footsteps fading into the distance. The weight of his absence settled upon Nikki's shoulders, a solemn reminder of the journey she now faced alone. She would embark on the path of self-discovery, confronting the tumultuous echoes of their past, and forging a future free from the chains of past hurts.

Nikki remained on the couch, her thoughts swirling in a tempest of conflicting emotions. The room felt heavy with memories, their ghosts dancing in the corners of her mind. But within the tangled labyrinth of heartache, a flicker of determination emerged—an ember of resilience, determined to rise from the ashes.

Nikki cautiously pushed open the door to George's office, her heart heavy with the weight of recent revelations. The room that had once been a sanctuary of creativity and passion now lay in disarray, scattered papers and photographs littering every surface. As her eyes swept across the chaos, a surge of emotions threatened to consume her.

This was the space where George had spent countless hours, lost in the world of his art. It was a place she had admired, cherishing the moments when she would quietly watch him sketch or paint, marveling at his talent. But now, as the truth unveiled itself layer by painful layer, she couldn't help but feel deceived. This room had harbored not only his artistic endeavors but also a secret life she had never suspected.

Rage coursed through Nikki's veins, fueled by a sense of betrayal and injustice. Her trembling hands reached down and clasped onto the baseball bat, discarded on the floor amidst the chaos. Gripping it tightly, she felt a primal surge of power and release. Without thinking, she swung the bat, the force behind each strike echoing her fury and heartbreak.

The sound of splintering wood and shattering glass filled the room as Nikki unleashed her pent-up anger, her blows raining down upon the remnants of George's hidden life. Photographs shattered, canvases crumpled, and the physical manifestations of his secrets disintegrated beneath her relentless assault.

But as the last fragments of her rage were spent, Nikki's strength faltered, and she crumpled to the ground, her body trembling with exhaustion. Collapsing into a heap, she buried her face in her hands, hot tears mingling with the dust and debris that surrounded her.

During the wreckage, a storm of emotions raged within her—grief, anger, confusion, and a profound sense of loss. The illusion of the life they had built together had shattered, revealing the painful truth she had been unknowingly shielded from. The weight of that truth pressed upon her, threatening to suffocate her spirit.

Slowly, Nikki lifted her head, her tear-stained face etched with determination. She knew that dwelling in the ruins of her shattered dreams would only prolong her agony. She had to find a way to move forward, to reclaim her own sense of identity and purpose.

With a heavy sigh, she wiped the tears from her face, smearing the traces of pain across her cheeks. The devastation behind her was a tangible reminder of the journey she had to embark upon— a journey of self-discovery, healing, and resilience.

Nikki stood up, her body aching, but her spirit rekindled with a flicker of strength.

The door to the office swung shut behind her, sealing away the wreckage of her past.

Nikki stepped out of her house and into the bright sunlight. The warmth of the sun on her skin felt like a balm after the emotional rollercoaster of the night before. As she walked down the street, she took a deep breath of the fresh air and felt the tension in her body almost start to melt away.

She had spent the morning alone, rooting through her feelings for George and the secrets she had found. It had been a difficult conversation, but in the end, it had felt like a weight had been lifted off her shoulders. She knew that there were still difficult days ahead, but for now, she felt like she could face them with a little more strength.

As she walked, Nikki took in the sights and sounds of the neighborhood around her. The sound of cars honking in the distance, the smell of freshly cut grass, and the chatter of people on the street all mixed into a symphony that felt like the soundtrack to her life.

She walked past a group of kids playing hopscotch on the sidewalk and couldn't help but smile. Their laughter was infectious, and for a moment, she felt like a kid again too. The world was a big and scary place, but moments like these reminded her that they could be anyone, anywhere.

Nikki leaned against her porch railing; the weight of weariness etched upon her face. It had been a long night, filled with tossing and turning, plagued by fragmented slumbers that danced just out of reach. As the morning sunlight filtered through the trees, casting dappled shadows upon her worn porch, she longed for a moment of respite, a moment to find solace within the confines of her home.

But fate had a different plan in store.

With a creaking gate, her elderly neighbor, Mrs. Patterson, shuffled toward her, her frail form bent with age. An air of unease clung to the air as the woman approached, her eyes filled with a mixture of curiosity and concern.

"Nikki, dear, I couldn't help but notice the noises and commotion last night," Mrs. Patterson ventured cautiously, her voice trembling with a fragile timbre.

Nikki sighed inwardly, the weight of exhaustion settling upon her shoulders. She was in no mood to entertain idle chatter or delve into the mysterious nocturnal happenings. Her patience, already frayed, threatened to unravel completely.

"Look, Mrs. Patterson, I'm really not in the mood for this right now," Nikki interjected, her voice tinged with a raw weariness. "I had a rough night, and I just want some peace and quiet. Can we discuss this another time?"

Mrs. Patterson recoiled, her features contorting with a blend of shock and offense. Her eyes, once filled with curiosity, now shimmered with wounded pride. The fragility of the moment hung heavy in the air, an unspoken tension that cast a pall over the porch.

Nikki's words, sharp and dismissive, lingered between them, a chasm that threatened to widen with each passing second. She had never intended to strike at her neighbor's vulnerability, but in her exhaustion, her sharp tongue had dealt an unintended blow.

A silence settled, punctuated only by the distant chirping of birds and the faint rustling of leaves. Mrs. Patterson, her face flushed with a mix of hurt and indignation, nodded stiffly.

"I... I apologize, Nikki," she whispered, her voice strained. "I didn't mean to intrude. I'll leave you be."

As her neighbor turned and retreated, Nikki felt a pang of regret twist within her gut. The weight of her own tiredness seemed a feeble excuse, a thin veil to mask the brusqueness of her response. She watched as Mrs. Patterson shuffled away, her figure growing smaller with each step.

In that solitary moment, Nikki realized the cost of her weariness, the toll it exacted upon those around her. She knew she would need to mend the breach, to seek forgiveness and understanding from her neighbor. But for now, as the echoes of her curt words reverberated within her, she stood alone on her porch, swallowed by a sea of remorse.

CHAPTER TEN.

N ikki stood still; her eyes fixed upon the unassuming facade of her house. A veil of contemplation cloaked her, casting a shadow across her features. The morning had been consumed by profound musings on the enigma of those who lived in the shadows, those who dared to traverse the treacherous terrain of duplicity. What must it be like, she wondered, to perpetually shroud a fragment of one's essence from the prying eyes of the world?

Whispers of clandestine existence reached her ears, tales of individuals leading lives of secrecy, juggling family's unseen and careers concealed. Such stories had nestled in the recesses of her mind, sowing seeds of curiosity. You see it every day, on the news. Someone's got a secret that just spills out like an oil slick.

What propelled these souls to hoard their true selves beneath layers of pretense? Was it the fear of judgment, or the burden of shame? Or perchance, a profound yearning to shield a vulnerable fragment of their being from the harsh light of reality?

George, her partner, had never been someone she suspected of leading a double life. Yet, as she delved into the depths of his intimate scribblings, an unsettling revelation gnawed at her core. The depths of his struggles—his clandestine skirmishes with depression, anxiety, and the relentless demands of his vocation—had been veiled from her gaze, concealed behind a carefully crafted facade. The gravity of his hidden battles, she now realized, had taken an insidious toll, shrouding him in an impenetrable cloak of isolation she had failed to fully comprehend.

Regret washed over her, its tendrils sinking deep within her heart. Memories surged forth, rousing a tumultuous mixture of guilt and introspection. How many times had she pushed him away, heedless of the silent storm raging within him? How often had she failed to truly listen, allowing his unvoiced anguish to drift away like whispers in the wind? Perhaps, had she been more attuned, more perceptive, she could have shared the weight of his burdens, offering solace and support. Perhaps, in some small measure, she could have kindled a transformative ember within his life.

Time drifted like fragments of a fading dream as she lingered in that moment of introspection, the weight of realization resting upon her shoulders. It dawned upon her that living a life of duality transcended more than just concealment from the world— you were constantly in a dance with yourself. It entailed a deliberate denial, an act of disowning an unwelcome fragment of existence, one too painful or inconvenient to acknowledge. The dual life, she discerned, was a path paved with loneliness and isolation—a journey embarked upon with the sole purpose of eluding the discomforting gaze of truth.

Nikki slipped silently off the porch. *Not a sound.* She felt the roughness and coolness of the sidewalk underneath her bare feet. It sent a small wake-up call to her brain, but she carried on, moving into a walking stance.

One step…after the other…

The morning sunlight painted a muted hue over the bustling streets of downtown Washington as Nikki tread wearily, her bare feet weary against the unforgiving pavement. Fatigue clung to her like a heavy shroud, burdening her every step.

Thoughts swirled in her mind, a cacophony of distractions that threatened to overwhelm her.

She had tasks to accomplish, and responsibilities to fulfill. Among them, the forgotten birthday present for her sister lingered at the fringes of her thoughts. But all she could summon was the image of George, his absence looming large in her consciousness. His memory wrapped around her like a suffocating embrace, consuming her thoughts and blurring her focus.

Seeking respite, she entered a crowded coffee shop and settled into a corner, seeking solace within the embrace of anonymity. She felt the weight of curious gazes upon her, their prying eyes dissecting her disheveled appearance, her haunted countenance. The whispers of secrets, concealed within the lives of those around her, whispered like distant echoes in her mind.

Grief, an invisible thread that bound humanity together, hovered in the air. She wondered how many people in that bustling café were harboring their own sorrows, their own private battles. The weight of collective mourning pressed upon her, a reminder that her anguish was not unique. She contemplated the silent struggles of others, the masks they wore to conceal their pain, and the unspoken stories that swirled beneath the surface.

Lost in her musings, she daydreamed about George's life beyond her reach, a clandestine existence she had never suspected. What secrets had he held? What unspoken desires had driven him? She allowed her mind to wander, painting vivid images of a hidden realm, until reality rudely intruded, snapping her back to the present.

She drained the remnants of her coffee cup, the bitter taste mingling with her thoughts. Rising from her seat, she felt a faint pang of unease, an unsettling sensation that she was being watched, pursued. Rationality reminded her that it was likely a product of her restless mind, yet a lingering paranoia persisted.

Undeterred, Nikki continued her journey through the city streets, a lone figure in a sea of faces. She quickened her pace, the rhythm of her footsteps resonating with a determination born of survival. The shadows of doubt trailed behind her, but she refused to succumb to their haunting whispers. For within her, a flicker of strength burned, an ember of resilience that would guide her through the labyrinth of uncertainty.

*

Nikki stepped into the bustling art gallery, the scent of creativity and inspiration filling the air. She wandered through the vibrant space, her eyes drawn to the kaleidoscope of colors and the myriad of emotions captured on canvas. Amongst the sea of artwork, one particular painting beckoned her with an irresistible pull.

She approached it tentatively, her gaze locked upon the masterpiece that bore George's name. It was the only painting of his that had ever made its way into a gallery, a testament to his talent that had remained hidden from the world. As Nikki stood before the artwork, time seemed to slow, the chatter of the crowd fading into the background, leaving her alone with the enigmatic strokes and captivating hues.

The painting spoke to her on a profound level, each brushstroke revealing a different facet of George's soul. There was a depth to it, a complexity that mirrored the conflicting emotions she had sensed within him. In its vibrant colors and textured layers, she glimpsed joy and melancholy, hope and despair, and the troubled truths that dwelled within his heart.

The central image, a solitary figure, held an air of mystery. Its eyes, filled with both longing and resignation, seemed to search for answers that eluded even the artist himself. Nikki found herself captivated; her own emotions entwined with the intricate layers of the painting. She saw her own struggles, her own hopes and fears reflected in the carefully crafted strokes of the brush.

Within the composition, Nikki sensed a delicate balance between light and darkness, a metaphor for the intricate dance between love and pain that George had carried within him. The painting spoke of a journey, of an artist's quest to understand the complexities of human existence, to capture the intangible moments that define our lives.

As Nikki stood there, absorbed in the artistry before her, she couldn't help but wonder about the untold stories concealed within George's work. What truths had he poured onto the canvas? What secrets had he hidden beneath layers of color and texture?

The conflicting meanings in the painting mirrored the conflicting emotions within herself. She was torn between her love for George and the realization that there were depths to him she had never fully comprehended. The artwork whispered of untold chapters, of hidden experiences that shaped the man she had married.

Emotions swirled within Nikki, a whirlwind of confusion, curiosity, and a longing for understanding. She yearned to unravel the enigma of George's art, to decipher the emotions woven into each brushstroke. Yet, she couldn't escape the apprehension that in uncovering the truths contained within the painting, she might uncover truths about George himself that could shatter the carefully constructed image she held of him.

With a sigh, Nikki stepped back from the painting, her eyes lingering on the complex masterpiece. It held a power over her, an invitation to explore the intricacies of her own relationship, her own perceptions of love and truth. The conflicting meanings it conveyed echoed the complexity of their lives together.

*

Nikki's footsteps echoed against the pavement as she continued to walk, her feet moving mechanically, guided by a mind lost in contemplation. The bustling town carried on around her, oblivious to the turmoil that churned within her. Happy couples strolled hand in hand, children laughed and played, and elderly individuals found solace in the warmth of shared memories.

As she observed the joyful scenes unfolding around her, Nikki couldn't help but feel a profound sense of isolation. Amidst the sea of faces, she wondered who among them would truly understand the depths of her thoughts, the conflicts that gnawed at her heart. Would anyone be able to sense her inner turmoil and offer a guiding hand, a comforting word?

With each passing couple, a pang of envy tugged at her. She yearned for the ease and simplicity that seemed to radiate from their interactions. She longed for someone to look into her eyes and understand the intricate emotions that churned within her. But as she watched the happy pairs, she couldn't help but question whether their outward bliss masked their own hidden struggles.

The laughter of children echoed in her ears, a reminder of the innocence and purity that seemed to elude her in this moment of introspection. She wondered if they held the key to unlocking the simplicity of life, if their unburdened minds could provide her with the clarity she sought. But deep down, she knew that the answers she sought were far more complex than the innocence of youth could comprehend.

The elderly figures she encountered carried with them a sense of wisdom, etched into the lines of their faces and the depth of their gaze. Nikki couldn't help but wonder if they had experienced the same conflicts and doubts that plagued her own heart. Were they, too, confronted with choices that required courage and sacrifice? Or had they found a way to navigate the turbulent waters of life and emerge with a sense of contentment? The weight of her husband George's secret family rested heavily on her mind. She felt a mix of emotions —confusion, anger, and a deep desire to uncover the truth.

Chapter Eleven.

A s she stared into the distance, contemplating her next move, a voice interrupted her reverie.

"Excuse me, dear, is this seat taken?" a gentle voice asked.

Nikki looked up to see a kindly elderly woman standing beside her table. Her wrinkled face wore a warm smile, and her eyes sparkled with a hint of mischief. Nikki shook her head and gestured for the woman to take a seat.

"My name is Elizabeth," the woman introduced herself, extending a hand.

"Nikki," she replied, shaking Elizabeth's hand. "Nice to meet you."

Elizabeth's eyes softened, and she lowered her voice. "I couldn't help but overhear your conversation with the barista.

I'm so sorry for your loss, dear. Losing someone you love is never easy."

Nikki appreciated Elizabeth's empathy and welcomed the opportunity to talk. "Thank you," she replied, her voice filled with gratitude. "It's been a difficult time for me."

"I can only imagine," Elizabeth said, her voice filled with genuine concern. "If you don't mind me asking, what brings you to this point in your journey?"

Nikki hesitated for a moment, unsure if she should trust a stranger with her secret. But something about Elizabeth's presence felt comforting, as if she had known her for years. So, she decided to share a condensed version of her story.

"I recently discovered some things about my late husband, and wanted to see what other secrets he kept," Nikki revealed, her voice tinged with sadness. "I'm trying to find out more about his past, to understand why he kept things from me."

Elizabeth nodded sympathetically; her eyes filled with understanding. "Sometimes, our loved ones carry secrets they believe are protecting us," she said gently. "But in the end, the truth always finds a way."

Nikki sighed, feeling a mix of frustration and determination. "I just don't know where to start. It's like trying to unravel a tangled web of lies."

Elizabeth leaned forward; her expression filled with wisdom. "Have you considered going to the archives?" she suggested. "Sometimes, the answers we seek are hidden in old records, newspaper clippings, or even interviews with those who knew our loved ones in the past."

Nikki's eyes widened with newfound hope. The idea of searching through archives seemed like a tangible way to uncover the truth. "I've never thought about that," she admitted. "But it sounds like a good place to start."

Elizabeth smiled warmly. "Trust your instincts, Nikki. Sometimes, the most unexpected encounters and avenues can lead us to the answers we seek."

Feeling a renewed sense of purpose, Nikki thanked Elizabeth for her guidance and bid her farewell. As she left, she couldn't help but feel a glimmer of hope. Perhaps the archives would hold the key to unlocking George's secret past.

*

Nikki was determined to dig deeper into George's past, hoping to uncover more information that could shed light on his secretive double life. Armed with determination, she set out to explore the archive—a treasure trove of historical records, newspaper clippings, and interviews from the time and place George claimed to have grown up.

As Nikki stepped into the dimly lit archive room, the musty scent of old papers filled her senses. She was greeted by rows upon rows of dusty shelves, holding the secrets of the past. With focused determination, she began her search, carefully handling each fragile document.

Her first stop was the newspaper clippings section. She meticulously scanned through articles, searching for any mention of George's name. After what seemed like hours of combing through the pages, Nikki's eyes finally caught a glimpse of something familiar. There it was—George's name, but it was only associated with local sports achievements. There was no mention of a second family or any other notable events.

Frustrated yet undeterred, Nikki turned her attention to old records, hoping to find some hidden connections. She carefully reviewed birth records, marriage certificates, and even school records. However, there was no trace of George's involvement with a second family or any information that hinted at his double life.

Feeling a sense of discouragement, Nikki took a moment to collect her thoughts. She reminded herself that the truth was often buried deep, requiring persistence to unveil. With renewed determination, she delved into the collection of interviews from the past, hoping to stumble upon a hidden gem.

As she meticulously went through the interviews, Nikki stumbled upon an intriguing article. It discussed an inappropriate relationship between an older woman and a younger man. Her heart skipped a beat as she pondered if this could be a piece of the puzzle she was seeking. However, the article did not mention any names, leaving her uncertain if it had any connection to George.

Realizing she needed more evidence to draw any conclusions, Nikki jotted down the details of the article and made a note to investigate further. She planned to interview individuals from that period who might have more insight or information about the scandalous affair.

Leaving the archive, Nikki carried a mix of anticipation and frustration. She had found glimpses of George's presence in the past, but nothing concrete enough to confirm his double life. Determined to leave no stone unturned, she knew that more interviews and investigations were needed to connect the dots and uncover the truth about George's hidden secrets.

*

Nikki stepped out of the archive and stumbled incidentally into a stranger... ... Nikki stood in disbelief as she stared at the figure standing before her. It was Junior, the very person she believed she had incapacitated in self-defense that fateful night. Her heart raced, unsure of what to expect from this unexpected encounter.

Junior's face bore remnants of the injuries he had sustained, but there was a determined look in his eyes. He approached Nikki cautiously, keeping a safe distance between them. A mix of emotions swirled within her—fear, anger, and even a tinge of sadness for the troubled young man who stood before her.

"Nikki," Junior began, his voice filled with a blend of remorse and desperation. "I know you must hate me for what I did, but I survived. I'm sorry for everything that happened."

Nikki's mind was a whirlwind of conflicting thoughts and emotions. She remembered the fear and the anger that consumed her during their encounter, but she also recognized the complexity of Junior's situation. Deep down, she knew he had been manipulated and controlled by Mama, just like she had been.

A part of her wanted to understand Junior's side of the story, to find some sort of closure and reconciliation. But another part of her, scarred by the traumatic events they had endured, hesitated to let him back into her life. She needed time and space to heal from the wounds that still haunted her.

"I appreciate your apology, Junior," Nikki replied, her voice trembling slightly. "But I need time to process everything. I'm not ready to open that door again."

Junior's face fell, disappointment etched across his features. He understood Nikki's reluctance, but he couldn't deny the hope that had welled up within him at the possibility of redemption and forgiveness.

"I understand," he murmured, his voice filled with resignation. "But remember, when the time's right, I'll be here. I'll be ready to face the consequences of my actions and make amends."

Nikki nodded, a mixture of emotions coursing through her. She felt a flicker of compassion for Junior, knowing that he had been entangled in a web of manipulation and abuse just like she had. But she also realized the importance of prioritizing her own healing and well-being.

As Junior walked away, leaving Nikki to grapple with the complex emotions swirling within her, she took a deep breath and reminded herself that she had made progress in her journey. She had uncovered George's secret family, confronted Mama, and sought answers from the archives. Now, it was time to focus on herself and rebuild her life.

With renewed determination, Nikki turned her gaze toward the future, ready to face whatever challenges lay ahead. She knew that healing would take time, but she was determined to emerge stronger and wiser from the shadows of her past.

CHAPTER TWELVE.

Four hours later she arrived at West Key Point, the other side of the neighborhood. The sun had started its descent, casting long shadows across the streets as she made her way towards Kayla's house. Each step felt heavier than the last, and dread weighed down her heart. She had been rehearsing the conversation in her mind, playing out different scenarios, but now that the moment was approaching, the weight of her secret seemed almost unbearable.

As she walked towards Kayla's house, the neighborhood seemed different. It had always been a place of familiarity and comfort, but now it appeared foreign to her. The houses she passed, once familiar landmarks, now seemed like strangers standing in judgment. She couldn't help but wonder what Kayla's reaction would be. Would she be angry?

Disappointed? Concerned? The uncertainty gnawed at her, intensifying her already heightened emotions.

Finally reaching Kayla's house, she hesitated for a moment outside the front gate.

She took in the changes that had occurred since her last visit. A tiny porch with colored glass had been added around the front door, giving the house a whimsical charm. Ruffled net curtains adorned each window, gently swaying in the breeze. The brass letterbox gleamed in the afternoon sunshine, a small detail that stood out amidst her turmoil.

Summoning her courage, she pressed the plastic doorbell and waited. The seconds felt like an eternity, her mind racing with anticipation and anxiety. Eventually, a harried woman opened the door, her forced smile revealing a hint of relief and exhaustion. The woman's apron, adorned with a "Love Is..." cartoon, seemed out of place now. An overpowering scent of caramel and gin wafted out from the house, mingling with the tension in the air.

"Your sister's out back, honey. You want to go around the... side?" the woman said, gesturing towards the garden.

Nikki suddenly became acutely aware of her appearance, realizing how she must have seemed to this stranger who was likely one of Kayla's colleagues. She stood barefoot, wearing a pink vest top and pajama shorts, her disheveled appearance a reflection of her emotional state. She nodded silently and made her way to the garden, her footsteps light on the soft grass.

As she turned the corner, she saw a gathering of people. They were friends and acquaintances of Kayla, mingling and laughing, unaware of the storm brewing within Nikki's heart. Their expressions shifted as they noticed her presence— dismay, surprise, and even awe filled their faces. It was as if her emotional turmoil had manifested itself physically, leaving her completely exposed.

"SIS!" Kayla's voice rang out, cutting through the noise of the gathering. She emerged from the crowd, seemingly appearing out of thin air, and hurriedly moved away from the party. With arms outstretched, she walked towards Nikki and enveloped her in a tight embrace. The concern and empathy in Kayla's embrace were palpable, overwhelming Nikki with a mix of gratitude and vulnerability.

"You look exhausted," Kayla said softly, pulling away slightly to study Nikki's face.

"Come on into the house... let's talk."

With a slightly tipsy lurch, Kayla took hold of Nikki's upper arm gently, guiding her into the kitchen. The room was filled with the remnants of the party, empty glasses and half-eaten appetizers strewn across the counters. Kayla's concern was evident as she studied Nikki's disheveled appearance.

"Nikki, what's happened, girl? Why are you barefoot? What's going on?" Kayla's voice trembled with worry.

Nikki sank into a chair at the kitchen table, exhaustion settling heavily upon her. She took a deep breath, summoning the strength to recount the events that had unfolded over the past few days. With trembling hands, she began to explain everything—the discoveries she had made, the hidden photographs and letters she had found in George's office. Kayla listened intently, her eyes widening with each revelation.

"Nikki, you can't be serious. George? That's impossible," Kayla said, her voice filled with a mix of disbelief and concern.

Nikki felt a surge of frustration rising within her. How could Kayla not believe her? She had irrefutable evidence, and yet her own sister seemed hesitant to accept the truth.

"I'm telling you, Kayla, it's true. I have the evidence at home... I just..." Nikki's voice trailed off, her frustration turning into regret as she realized she had impulsively thrown George's notebook in the trash during her haste to leave the house.

Kayla sighed deeply, her brow furrowing as she tried to make sense of the situation.

"Nikki, I think you're just still grieving. Maybe you're just seeing what you want to see.

Maybe it's a distraction from dealing with Dad's death."

Nikki's anger flared up, burning hot within her. How could Kayla dismiss her like this? She stood up abruptly, the chair toppling over behind her. "I can't believe you're not taking this seriously! I need to go."

Without waiting for a response, Nikki stormed out of the house, her footsteps echoing through the empty hallway. The guests gathered in the living room were left in stunned silence, their chatter replaced by an awkward stillness.

As she stepped out into the weak sunshine that was gleaming through a rupture in the thick clouds, she had never been more conscious of the change in her fate. She was alone now, completely. Humiliated, furious, groaning in agony, Nikki dragged herself along the sidewalk, barely pulling herself out of the path of any oncoming traffic.

She heard a car pull up on the left side of her.

Nikki moved to avoid him, but he pushed open the passenger door to block her way.

"No, you don't. You're not getting out of it that easy. Get in."

Nikki's heart raced as she saw blood seeping through Junior's shirt and on his hands. She took a step back, but he told her once again to get in the car.

Nikki hesitated, unsure if she should trust him. But then she noticed the urgency in his voice and the certainty in his eyes. Finally dropping down into the passenger seat, she slammed the door shut behind her and

"Where are we going?" "We are going to meet the family."

She was helpless to do anything else.

"Okay," she said, trying to sound calm. "Let's go."

The car pulled away from the curb, and Nikki tried to steady her breathing. She couldn't believe she was willingly getting into a car with a man covered in blood, heading to meet a family she had never even heard of before.

But she knew she had to stay strong and keep her wits about her. George had always told her to be prepared for anything, and now was the time to put that advice to use.

As they drove into the night, Nikki couldn't help but wonder what she had gotten herself into. She felt a sense of dread wash over her, but she also felt George's presence beside her, giving her strength.

She knew she had to be strong for whatever was coming next.

*

Nikki sat in the passenger seat of Junior's car, her heart racing with fear and anticipation. She had no idea where they were headed, and the darkness outside only added to her unease.

Junior was driving in silence, and she couldn't read anything from his expression.

As they continued to drive deeper into the night, Nikki couldn't help but feel like she was being taken to meet some kind of unsavory fate. She wondered who this mysterious "family" was that Junior had referred to, and what they wanted from her.

But then, she felt a familiar presence surrounding her. It was George, her late husband. She could feel his calming energy and his protective embrace, even though he wasn't physically there.

Nikki closed her eyes and took a deep breath, feeling George's strength flow through her. She steeled herself for whatever was to come, knowing that she wasn't alone.

As they drove on, the darkness refused to lift, and Nikki could only see the faint outline of a house in the distance. It was a large, imposing building, and it sent shivers down her spine.

Junior pulled the car to a stop in front of the house, and Nikki's heart began to pound with fear. She could feel George's presence urging her to stay strong.

CHAPTER THIRTEEN.

Nikki stepped out of the car, her eyes scanning the desolate surroundings. They had arrived at an isolated location, far away from any signs of civilization. Gravel paths wound through overgrown vegetation, casting an eerie shadow over the landscape. The only visible structure was a dilapidated house, standing with a sense of melancholic abandonment, it is peeling paint and crooked roof hinting at a forgotten past.

A chill ran down Nikki's spine as Junior approached her, his rough grip forcing her to walk towards the house. Fear gripped her heart, causing it to race uncontrollably. She closed her eyes for a moment, seeking solace in her memories of George—his love, his protection. Though he was no longer physically present, she held onto the belief that his spirit would guide and shield her in this dark moment.

As they neared the house, a woman emerged from the worn wooden doorway. She appeared to be in her late fifties to mid-sixties, with gentle eyes and a warm smile. Yet, there was an undercurrent of something strange that Nikki couldn't quite put her finger on. The woman introduced herself as Mama, and a surge of recognition washed over Nikki. This was the woman George had been involved with before he met her—the one he had never spoken about.

Mama embraced Junior warmly, their familiarity palpable. Nikki felt like an outsider, an intruder stumbling upon a clandestine family gathering. She tried to mask her discomfort, putting on a brave face while battling the uneasy sensation that gnawed at her.

"Come inside, come inside," Mama beckoned, leading them through the creaking door. Nikki cast one last glance at the weathered exterior, an unspoken prayer for strength whispered under her breath, before stepping over the threshold and into the mysterious house.

The interior was dimly lit, with the soft glow of fading daylight streaming through dusty windows. The air carried a musty scent, a mingling of memories and neglect. The floors creaked beneath their footsteps, as if whispering secrets of their own. Nikki's gaze swept across the room, taking in the mismatched furniture, worn-out rugs, and faded photographs adorning the walls—a visual representation of a forgotten past.

Mama guided them into a sitting area, inviting them to take a seat on a threadbare couch. Nikki couldn't help but notice the collection of trinkets and curiosities scattered around the room, each with its own story waiting to be told. She wondered what secrets this house held, what hidden chapters of George's life would be revealed within its weathered walls.

Junior settled into an armchair; his body relaxed as if he were in a familiar sanctuary. Mama busied herself in the kitchen, the clinking of dishes and the aroma of simmering spices wafting through the air. Nikki's unease grew, her senses attuned to the dissonance that lingered beneath the surface of this unexpected reunion.

Lost in her thoughts, she didn't realize that Mama had returned, bearing a tray of steaming tea. She placed it on the coffee table, the warmth radiating like a beacon of solace amid uncertainty. Nikki accepted the cup with trembling hands, the porcelain surface offering a momentary respite from the chill that had settled deep within her bones.

As the liquid touched her lips, memories flooded her mind—moments shared with George, laughter, and whispered promises of forever. She wondered how she had arrived at this juncture, navigating a labyrinth of secrets and betrayal. But she knew that to uncover the truth, she needed to confront Mama, to delve into the shadows of her past.

As they all sat down to dinner, the tension in the air became palpable, casting a heavy cloud over the room. Nikki attempted to engage in small talk, hoping to steer the conversation away from the uneasy topic of George.

"How's things, Junior?" Mama asked, her tone tinged with a mix of curiosity and veiled resentment, as she took a bite of her mashed potatoes.

Junior shrugged, avoiding eye contact. "Fine, fine," he muttered, his words lacking conviction.

Nikki seized the opportunity to shift the focus, directing her attention towards Mama.

"How's your garden coming along? Junior mentioned that you've been working on it.

It must be quite beautiful."

Mama's response was curt, her voice betraying a hint of frustration. "It's coming along, I suppose. But it's not easy taking care of everything by myself."

Nikki sensed the lingering resentment in Mama's words, the unspoken accusation that George had been taken away from her. She knew that Mama viewed George as someone who belonged to her, and she couldn't shake the feeling that she had unwittingly become the target of Mama's misplaced anger.

Feeling the weight of Mama's unspoken words, Nikki gathered her courage and decided to broach a delicate subject.

"I was going through George's things the other day," she began, her voice gentle and cautious. "And I found some old pictures of..." Mama's face hardened, the lines etching deeper as she interrupted with a sharp tone. "I remember everything. I don't need pictures," she retorted, her eyes flashing with unresolved emotions. "I remember when you first came into our lives, and he started spending all his time with you. He forgot about us."

Nikki's heart sank as she listened to Mama's bitter words. She understood the pain and resentment that Mama carried, the belief that she had been abandoned by George. But Nikki also knew that the truth was far more complex, that George had loved both Mama and his children deeply.

"I'm sure that's not true," Nikki interjected, her voice infused with a mix of empathy and defense. "I'm sure he loved his children very much. And from what I read, he never forgot about you."

Mama's gaze hardened; her eyes locked with Nikki's. "Then why did he leave?" she demanded, her voice rising with a surge of raw emotion. "Why did he leave us for you?"

A pang of guilt gripped Nikki's chest, as she grappled with the weight of Mama's accusation. She knew that Mama's pain stemmed from a place of hurt, from a sense of abandonment that she couldn't fully comprehend. Yet, she also knew that George's decision had been a complex one, driven by circumstances and emotions that couldn't be easily summarized.

"He didn't leave you for me," Nikki whispered, her voice trembling with a mixture of remorse and conviction. "He loved us both. And he never meant to hurt anyone."

Mama scoffed, pushing her plate away with a sharp movement. "I don't want to talk about him anymore," she declared, her voice filled with a mixture of resignation and bitterness. "He's gone, and he's not coming back. And neither are you if you can't respect that."

Nikki felt a lump forming in her throat, a whirlwind of conflicting emotions threatening to overwhelm her. The weight of Mama's words, coupled with her own guilt and the ache of loss, bore down upon her. She couldn't help but feel a sense of despair, as she realized the depth of Mama's pain and the gulf that seemed to separate them.

Nikki's heart pounded in her chest as Mama's anger reached its boiling point. She had witnessed Mama's outbursts before, but this time was different. It was as if something inside Mama had snapped, unleashing a wave of rage and resentment.

"You need to learn your place, girl," Mama spat, her words laced with venom. "Junior, teach her a lesson."

Nikki's eyes widened in terror as Junior, his face contorted with anger, abruptly stood up from the table.

Without a word, he seized her arm and yanked her forcefully, dragging her up the stairs.

"Junior, stop!" Nikki pleaded, her voice quivering with fear, but her pleas fell on deaf ears. He propelled her into a dark room and slammed the door shut behind them, leaving her alone in the suffocating darkness.

Nikki's heart raced; her breath quickened as panic coursed through her veins. She had always harbored a fear of the dark, and being trapped in a room like this amplified her terror to its peak. Her trembling hands fumbled desperately in the darkness, seeking anything to hold onto, but she found only emptiness.

She fought to maintain her composure, attempting to regulate her breathing and steady her racing thoughts, but the whirlwind of questions tormented her. Why was Mama so consumed by anger? What had she done wrong to deserve this? And what awaited her at the hands of Junior?

Footsteps outside the door shattered the oppressive silence, causing Nikki's heart to leap into her throat. She pressed herself against the cold, unforgiving wall, desperate to make herself as inconspicuous as possible.

The footsteps ceased, replaced by the chilling sound of Junior's voice piercing through the heavy silence.

"You need to learn to respect Mama," he admonished, his tone low and menacing. "She's been through a lot, and she doesn't need you coming in here and stirring things up."

Nikki wanted to speak, to plead her case and assure Junior that she didn't intend to cause trouble. But her voice failed her in the face of fear, the words lodged like a lump in her throat.

"Open the door, Junior," she implored, her voice barely a whisper, filled with desperation. "Please, I don't want to be here anymore."

A prolonged silence ensued, amplifying Nikki's anxiety and the haunting uncertainty of her situation.

"It's too late," Junior finally responded, his words dripping with resignation.

Tears welled up in Nikki's eyes as remorse consumed her. "I'm sorry," she murmured, her voice carrying the weight of genuine regret. "I didn't mean to upset you. I just wanted to know the truth, same as you."

Junior scoffed, his voice brimming with bitterness. "You're always causing trouble," he retorted, his words filled with disdain. "Just stay in there until we're ready to deal with you, okay? We don't need your drama."

The sound of heavy footsteps receded, indicating Junior's departure from the vicinity. Nikki stood in the dark, her senses heightened, trying to discern any trace of their presence. Gradually, the realization settled upon her that she was truly alone in that foreboding room, left to confront her fears and await an uncertain fate.

Chapter Fourteen.

Nikki slowly opened her eyes, wincing. As her vision cleared, she realized she was in an unfamiliar room. She tried to move her arms and legs, but they felt heavy and unresponsive. A wave of pain washed over her, and she gasped, realizing that the pain was constant, throbbing beneath the surface.

Trying to push past the haze in her mind, Nikki initially struggled to remember what happened to her. She vaguely recalled sitting down to dinner, and arguing, but after that, everything was a blur. It felt like she'd been drugged or hit over the head, but she couldn't remember how or why.

As the pain ebbed and flowed, Nikki's thoughts drifted to her late husband George. Memories of their marriage flashed through her mind, and she tried to hold onto them, as they felt like the only thing grounding her in that moment.

Suddenly, Nikki sat up, gasping in pain. Her eyes scanned the dark room, trying to make sense of her surroundings. In the corner, she could make out what looked like a shadowy figure. She blinked a few times, trying to clear her vision, but the figure remained. Fear gripped her as she wondered who or what it could be.

Panic began to set in as she realized she was trapped and at the mercy of whoever put her there.

Nikki's eyes darted around the room, trying to find something to help her escape. It was then that she noticed a horrendous smell. It was a mix of burnt skin and something else she couldn't quite place. The odor made her gag, and she realized that whatever was causing the smell had slowly dissipated, leaving her on her own. Without smells, without light, without everything.

Nikki squinted her eyes, trying to get a better look at the figure in the corner. As her vision cleared, she realized with a jolt that it was not a stranger standing there but her late husband, George. The realization hit her hard, and she felt a lump form in her throat.

She had known George to be dead for almost a year now, so it was impossible for him to be standing there. Nikki quickly dismissed the thought, realizing that it must have been just another one of her hallucinations, this time brought on by the stress of her situation.

"George?" she whispered; her voice hoarse from misuse.

The figure didn't respond, and Nikki realized that it was just a figment of her imagination. She tried to ignore it, but the hallucination was persistent in its stoic silence, and she couldn't help but feel strangely comforted by its presence.

"Tell me, is this real? Or am I somewhere you can't even find me?" Nikki asked the hallucination, hoping for a response.

The figure remained silent, but Nikki felt like she could almost sense a response from it. She decided to take the chance and strike up a conversation.

"I miss you so much, George," she cried, tears streaming down her face. "I don't know how to go on without you."

As she spoke, the pain in her body subsided, and Nikki found herself feeling more at ease. She spoke to the hallucination for what seemed like hours, pouring out her heart and soul.

As she sat there, lost in thought, a childhood memory came flooding back to her. She remembered the time when she was just six years old, and she had gone on a camping trip with her family. It was the first time she had ever slept in a tent, and she had been both excited and scared.

She remembered waking up early in the morning to the sound of birds singing outside. She had poked her head out of the tent and seen her parents sitting around the campfire, drinking coffee and talking quietly. She had crawled out of the tent and gone to sit with them, feeling the warmth of the fire on her face.

Her mother had made her a cup of hot chocolate, and her father had pulled her onto his lap. They had sat there, watching the sunrise together, while her mother told her stories about when she was a little girl.

Nikki smiled to herself as she remembered how safe and loved she had felt in that moment. It was a memory that she had carried with her all her life, a reminder of a time when things were simpler and easier.

She took a deep breath and closed her eyes, letting the memory wash over her. For a few moments, she felt like that little girl again, safe and loved in the embrace of her parents.

*

Her thoughts drifted back to the day she met George.

It was a hot summer day, and Nikki was running late for a meeting. She rushed down the busy streets, dodging tourists and businessmen. As she turned the corner, she almost collided with a tall, good-looking man.

"Whoa there," he said, a smile spreading across his face.

"Sorry," Nikki replied, feeling a bit flustered.

"No worries. Are you okay?"

"I'm fine, thank you. I'm just running late."

"Me too," the man said, laughing. "My name is George, by the way." "I'm Nikki," she replied, smiling back at him.

They chatted for a few minutes, exchanging pleasantries and small talk. Nikki couldn't help but notice how charming and easygoing George was. She felt at ease in his company, as if they had known each other for years.

As they'd said their goodbyes and went their separate ways, Nikki couldn't shake the feeling that she had just met someone special. And she was right. George soon became a close friend and confidante, and eventually, something more.

Nikki warmed herself, lost in the memory of that chance encounter.

*

She thought back to the last time she had seen her husband George, alive and well. He had been ill, but they had thought he might recover. She had hoped against hope that he would be all right, that he would come back to her, and they would live a long and happy life together. But it was not meant to be.

The memory of George's last words to her still rang in her ears. "I love you," he had said, as he walked out the door for the last time. She had clung to those words, as if they were the only thing left in the world that mattered. But they had not been enough to keep him alive.

Nikki sighed and rubbed her temples, trying to ease the headache that was starting to form. She wished that she could go back in time, to that moment when George had said those words, and hold onto him forever. But she knew that was impossible.

George was gone, and she was stuck here, in this dark and dingy room, with no way out.

*

Hours, minutes, fruitlessly scrambling by... ...She was in nothingness.

A void. A void she was all too familiar with.

It tasted so similar to *grief.*

She lay for several minutes looking at the narrow strip of light under the door. Then she moved and tried to feel how exhausted she was, how tight the emotional bonds were. She could pull herself a bit, but the darkness and the exertion she'd been through grew taut immediately. She relaxed. She lay completely still, staring at nothing.

She waited. She fantasized about an open window and a safe route home.

She saw, in her imagination, the house drenched with flames. She could physically feel the heat on her back, as she moved away, towards home. She shook herself. She rattled. She opened her eyes and selected a spot. George was there, waiting for her. She heard him say something but shut her ears and didn't listen to the words. She saw the expression on his face as she moved across one part of the room. She heard the scraping sound of sulfur against the floorboards. It sounded like a drawn-out thunderclap. She saw the darkness overtake.

She steeled herself.

She didn't want that night to be the night she died.

*

Nikki's body slumped against the cold, unforgiving wall of the dark room. Her trembling hands clutched at her side, the source of a searing pain that radiated through her body. She could feel her consciousness slipping, her senses growing hazy.

Gasping for breath, Nikki fought to stay awake, to resist the lure of unconsciousness. She knew that succumbing to the darkness meant relinquishing any control she had over her situation. She couldn't let that happen. She had to find a way out, to escape the confines of this suffocating room.

With every ounce of strength, she could muster, Nikki forced herself to stand upright. The room spun around her, the darkness seeming to close in, but she refused to yield. She took faltering steps toward the door, her body swaying unsteadily with each movement.

The pain in her side intensified, causing her to wince with each breath. It felt as if a thousand knives were slicing through her, shredding her insides.

*

In the haze of consciousness, Nikki's eyes flickered open to a surreal sight. Standing before her, as if materialized from her deepest desires, was George. His presence seemed strangely solid, defying the boundaries of her perception. Was this a hallucination, a figment of her delirious mind? She couldn't be certain, but she clung to this ethereal vision, desperate for comfort and reassurance.

With a tender smile, George approached her, his hand gently reaching out to rub her head. The touch sent waves of warmth cascading through Nikki's body, momentarily easing her pain. She felt a flicker of hope, a fleeting sense of security in his presence.

In a surge of affection, Nikki leaned forward and placed a gentle kiss on George's cheek. But as her lips made contact, a peculiar shift occurred. George's expression changed, his features contorting with a mix of surprise and unease. He took a step back, his eyes clouded with a perplexed intensity.

"Nikki," he muttered, his voice laden with a mixture of longing and sorrow. "I can't stay. You know that."

Confusion washed over Nikki. Her fragile hold on reality wavered as George retreated to a corner of the room, pacing back and forth like a restless specter. She struggled to comprehend the dichotomy between his solid presence moments ago and his ephemeral existence now.

"George, please," she pleaded, her voice barely a whisper, laced with desperation. "I need you. I don't understand what's happening. Help me."

George's movements faltered; his gaze fixed on the floor. His face bore the weight of an unspoken burden, and for a fleeting moment, Nikki caught a glimpse of vulnerability in his eyes.

"I wish I could," he murmured, his voice tinged with regret. "But I'm trapped too, caught between realms. I can't change what has been, or what is to come."

As George's words sank in, Nikki felt a pang of sorrow pierce her heart. This vision of George, as tangible as it seemed, was merely a fleeting respite from her harsh reality.

Her mind struggled to reconcile the contradiction of his presence with the knowledge that he was gone.

Tears welled up in Nikki's eyes as she watched George's restless pacing, a silent reminder of the barriers that separated them. In her vulnerability, she clung to the memories they had shared, the love they had nurtured. But she also recognized the importance of letting go, of finding her own strength amidst the darkness.

CHAPTER FIFTEEN.

S everal silent minutes stretched between Nikki and the enigmatic figure she had mistaken for George. Emotions surged within her, tears streaming down her face while she intermittently tried to compose herself. She avoided meeting his gaze, unable to bear the weight of her confusion and the pain of their shattered connection.

"What?" Nikki finally managed to utter, her voice quivering with a mixture of anger and sorrow. The sight of him standing there, seemingly unperturbed, only intensified her frustration.

He offered her a gentle smile, a glimmer of warmth that clashed with the tumultuous emotions swirling inside her. In that moment, a sudden urge to laugh bubbled up within Nikki, an ironic reaction to the absurdity of their circumstances.

"Are you going to stand there all day?" she asked, attempting to mask her vulnerability with a veneer of irritation.

His smile widened; his eyes filled with an enigmatic spark. "No," he replied, his voice laced with a hint of playfulness. "I just wanted to show you the truth."

Curiosity mingled with apprehension as he approached Nikki, extending his hand toward her. She hesitated for a moment before tentatively reaching out, her fingers brushing against his palm. To her astonishment, his touch felt solid, undeniably real.

"Nikki," he began, his voice gentle but carrying an air of urgency. "There's something you need to know."

He handed her a photograph, her trembling hands grasping it tightly. As she glanced at the image, her heart skipped a beat. It was a picture of Mama, George, and the figure who had been masquerading as George himself. In the background, she noticed a subtle difference, a detail that shattered the illusion.

The truth unfurled before her eyes like a rapid-fire montage. Her mind raced to make sense of it all. The realization struck with an unsettling force—this person before her, who resembled George so eerily, was not him.

The weight of the revelation crushed Nikki's spirit, leaving her hollow and vulnerable. Fear welled up within her, a plea for this imposter to stay away, to release her from this twisted game of deception.

"Please..." she pleaded, her voice quivering with a mixture of confusion and anguish.

"I don't know who you are, but please, stay away from me."

"Nikki," he whispered, his voice tinged with a blend of sorrow and understanding.

"PLEASE!" she cried out, her plea echoing through the room, a desperate plea to protect herself from further deceit and confusion.

A tense silence enveloped them, the air was heavy with unspoken truths and shattered illusions. Nikki's heart pounded in her chest, her breaths coming in shallow gasps as she confronted the devastating reality before her. With each passing second, the chasm between truth and deception grew wider, leaving her adrift in a sea of uncertainty.

In the midst of her despair, a flicker of strength ignited within Nikki. Determination welled up within her, fueling her resolve to uncover the tangled web of lies that had ensnared her. She yearned for the truth, no matter how painful it might be, to emerge from the shadows and bring clarity to her shattered reality.

Nikki's heart raced inside her chest as the man approached her, his striking resemblance to her late husband George sending shivers down her spine. It was as though

George's ghost had materialized before her; his features etched onto this stranger's face. Fear gripped her tightly, threatening to paralyze her every move. But as he drew nearer, something in his expression softened, and he extended his hands in a reassuring gesture, a gesture that mirrored the tenderness she had once known so well.

"It's okay, Nikki," his voice, gentle and soothing, broke through the haze of uncertainty that clouded her mind. "I'm not here to hurt you."

Nikki's eyes widened; her gaze fixed on this enigmatic figure. Confusion mixed with her fear, a tumultuous storm brewing within her. Who was this man? How did he know her name? And why did he resemble George so strikingly? The questions swirled around her; demanding answers that seemed elusive.

His voice, calm yet filled with a hint of sadness, cut through the silence once again, seeking to allay her fears. "My name is Omar," he revealed, his eyes searching hers for understanding. "I'm George's other son. Junior and I were brought up to believe that he abandoned us, but that's not the truth. There were other things at play."

The weight of his words hung heavily in the air, the revelation hitting Nikki like a thunderbolt. Another son? Hidden secrets? The very foundation of her reality trembled, threatening to crumble beneath her. A kaleidoscope of emotions washed over her—surprise, disbelief, and a glimmer of hope intertwined in a complex dance.

Tentatively, Nikki found her voice. "George... had another son? Why was this kept from me? From everyone?"

Omar sighed; the burdens of a hidden past etched into the lines on his face. "It's a long and painful story, Nikki. One that we need to unravel together. George never wanted to abandon either of his families, but circumstances conspired against him. There were powerful forces at work, secrets that threatened to tear our lives apart."

Nikki's mind raced, trying to process the enormity of what she was hearing. The man standing before her was not an impostor or a figment of her imagination. He was flesh and blood, connected to George in a way she had never fathomed. The web of deception and the untold chapters of George's life slowly unraveled before her, and she realized that there was more to her late husband than she had ever known.

Overwhelmed by conflicting emotions, Nikki felt a mixture of anger, grief, and an unexpected surge of curiosity. She yearned to understand the truth that had been withheld from her for so long.

"I want to know," Nikki said with determination, her voice quivering slightly but resolute. "I want to uncover the truth, Omar. I want to understand who George really was, and why we were kept in the dark."

As she looked into Omar's eyes, she saw a tenderness there that reminded her so much of George. She felt conflicted, unsure of what to think or feel.

Omar reached out and took her hand, his touch gentle and comforting.

"I know this must be hard for you, Nikki," he said softly. "But I want you to know that I was never trying to replace George. I just wanted to meet you and see for myself what kind of person you are."

Nikki felt tears prickling at the corners of her eyes as she looked at Omar, overwhelmed by his kindness and sincerity. She knew that she needed to talk to him more, to understand what had really happened between Mama and George.

"Omar," she said, her voice barely above a whisper. "Can you tell me what really happened between Mama and George?"

Nikki listened intently as Omar shared the story of Mama and George's past. She couldn't believe what she was hearing. The image she had of George was shattered, and she felt angry and hurt that he had kept such a big secret from her.

George was a young man of seventeen, his presence a constant in the house he called home. Mama, known to him then as Thea, had been a friend of his parents, an enigmatic figure who possessed maturity beyond her years. The age gap between them casts a veil of intrigue over their interactions, drawing them into a delicate dance of friendship.

In those early days, George and Mama formed a connection that went beyond conventional boundaries. They found solace in each other's company, their conversations a blend of intellectual stimulation and shared interests. It was a relationship built on mutual understanding and trust, their friendship becoming an oasis amidst the chaos of their respective lives.

As time passed, a shift occurred within the dynamic between them. Then, with a fervent longing hidden beneath her composed exterior, began to see George through a different lens. She felt a pull toward him, a desire that blossomed in the hidden corners of her heart. She yearned for a love that defied the constraints of age and convention, willing to risk everything for a chance of happiness.

With trepidation, Thea revealed her true feelings to George, stepping into the realm of secrecy and clandestine affairs. She sought to pursue a relationship with him, shrouded in the shadows, away from prying eyes. But George, despite his youth and the allure of forbidden fruit, remained steadfast in his principles.

He had been raised with the values of integrity and respect, instilled within him by his parents. George understood the gravity of Mama's proposition, recognizing the potential consequences of their forbidden liaison. Though tempted by the allure of adventure and passion, he knew deep down that secret affairs were not the path he wished to tread.

With a heavy heart, George made the difficult decision to decline Mama's advances. He strove to maintain his integrity, clinging to the image of the gentleman he aspired to become. It was a choice made not out of cruelty or indifference, but out of a commitment to his own moral compass.

The rejection, no matter how gently delivered, cast a shadow over their once blossoming friendship. Thea, her heart bruised by the weight of unrequited love, withdrew into herself, burying the embers of desire beneath layers of stoicism. Their interactions, once filled with laughter and shared dreams, became tinged with a palpable tension, an unspoken reminder of what could have been.

The night was alive with the vibrant energy of the block party, laughter and music filling the air. George's parents had opened their doors to friends and neighbors, creating a lively atmosphere that seemed to drown out the troubles of the outside world. Amidst the revelry, George found himself caught in an unsettling encounter that would forever change his perception of trust and betrayal.

Thea, once a friend of his parents, now wore a different mask, intoxicated by the spirits that flowed freely throughout the gathering. Her intentions had become clouded, her inhibitions eroded by the alcohol coursing through her veins. Unbeknownst to George, a dark storm was brewing, and he would soon find himself at its merciless center.

Polite as ever, George gracefully sidestepped Thea's advances, aware of the boundaries that lay between them. He stood firm in his conviction, refusing to succumb to temptation or compromise his principles. Yet, Thea was relentless, driven by desires that clouded her judgment. Ignoring George's clear rejections, she resorted to manipulation, weaving a web of deception that would ensnare them both.

As the night wore on, Thea resorted to a sinister strategy. She took advantage of George's vulnerability, tricking him with drink after drink, exploiting his weakened state. George, unaware of her true intentions, found himself slipping into a haze of intoxication, his inhibitions fading with each sip.

In his muddled state, George's guard waned, and Thea seized her opportunity. While he was too inebriated to fully consent, she took him upstairs and they slept together. It was an act of betrayal, a breach of trust that cut deeper than any physical wound.

*

The morning light pierced through the curtains, casting a pale glow upon the room. George awoke, his mind clouded with remnants of the previous night's tumultuous encounter. As he turned to face Thea, the weight of unresolved tensions hung heavy in the air.

Silence filled the room, pregnant with unspoken words. George's gaze met Thea's, and within their eyes, a battle raged between accusation and denial. The events of the previous evening had left a bitter residue, staining their relationship with doubt and mistrust.

Words spilled forth, laced with anger and frustration. Thea, stubborn and unyielding, attempted to twist the truth, painting a distorted picture of the events that had transpired. George, grappling with his own confusion and guilt, defended himself against her manipulative accusations.

Days turned into weeks, and weeks into months. Thea's revelation shattered their fragile equilibrium, tearing through the fabric of George's carefully constructed life. The news of her pregnancy with his child carried a weight that both thrilled and terrified him. In the depths of his soul, a sense of responsibility took hold, urging him to support Thea from a distance, to shield her and the unborn child from further harm.

Years passed as George silently carried the burden of his secret, navigating a treacherous path of hidden support and unspoken longing. Thea, skilled in the art of manipulation, seized every opportunity to control the narrative, exploiting George's hidden involvement for her own gain.

In a tragic turn of events, Thea's web of deceit reached beyond her grasp, entangling George's unsuspecting parents. With calculated precision, she wove a tale of coercion and forced financial dependency, painting George as the villain in a twisted plot. Their hearts heavy with betrayal, George's parents chose to believe Thea's fabrications, severing the once-unbreakable bond between parent and child.

Broken and wounded, George made the painful decision to escape the suffocating grip of his past. He sought solace and a fresh start in Washington, a city where the echoes of his former life could be muted. It was there, amidst the buzzing streets and bustling crowds, that fate led him to Nikki.

In the delicate dance of their blossoming relationship, George found a sliver of hope, a chance at redemption and a glimpse of the love that had eluded him for so long. Fearful of tarnishing this newfound connection, he shielded Nikki from the haunting shadows of his past, burying his secrets deep within the recesses of his soul.

Yet, even as George tried to bury the past, it continued to claw at his conscience. The persistent presence of Mama, Thea's sons, weighed heavily upon his heart, a constant reminder of the turmoil that still lingered beneath the surface. Harassment seeped into his life, a reminder of the web of manipulation that continued to ensnare him.

Time passed, leaving behind a trail of untold stories and unanswered questions. The weight of guilt and shame pressed upon George's shoulders, eroding his spirit with each passing day. The pain of his untimely death, claimed by an unforeseen aneurysm, echoed through the hearts of those who knew him, leaving behind a legacy marred by the shadows of betrayal.

CHAPTER SIXTEEN.

Nikki's admission hung heavy in the air, an unspoken acknowledgment of the tangled web of deceit that had ensnared them all. Omar met her gaze, his eyes filled with a mix of understanding and compassion. He could sense the turmoil within her, the weight of guilt and confusion threatening to overwhelm her.

"No, Nikki, it's not your fault," Omar reassured her, his voice gentle yet firm. "Mama had a way of distorting the truth, of manipulating those around her. It's only natural that her lies would leave a mark on your perception. But now that we know the truth, we can find a way to move forward, to heal."

Nikki nodded, the weight of her misplaced judgment and lingering guilt slowly lifted from her shoulders. She had been a pawn in Mama's game, an unwitting participant in a narrative she never fully understood. But now, with Omar by her side, she felt a renewed sense of purpose—a determination to uncover the depths of George's past and find closure for their shared pain.

Omar leaned forward; his voice laced with sincerity. "Nikki, I want you to know that George loved you deeply. Despite the secrets he carried, he cherished the time he spent with you. His decision to shield you from the truth was driven by a misguided sense of shame and a desire to protect you from Mama's toxic influence."

Tears welled in Nikki's eyes as the weight of George's love and sacrifice washed over her. She had loved him fiercely, and to learn that he had endured years of torment on her behalf tore at her heart. In that moment, she vowed to honor his memory by uncovering the full truth, by exposing Mama's web of lies for what it truly was.

Omar reached out, gently taking Nikki's hand in his own. "We're in this together, Nikki. I've spent years fighting against Mama's manipulation, trying to untangle the threads of truth from her deceit. And now, with you by my side, we can confront her, expose her lies, and seek justice for George and ourselves."

A newfound determination coursed through Nikki's veins. She realized that she had a choice—to be defined by the darkness of Mama's actions or to rise above it, to forge a path of healing and redemption. George's untimely death had left wounds that may never fully heal, but together, Nikki and Omar would strive to find solace and closure.

Nikki sat in stunned silence, taking in Omar's words. Her mind was reeling, trying to make sense of all the new information. George had been a good man, after all. He had been forced into a terrible situation, and he had done everything he could to protect his family.

As she looked at Omar, she realized how much he looked like his father. It was as if George's spirit was still with them, guiding them through this difficult time.

"Thank you for telling me the truth," Nikki said softly, breaking the silence. "I had no idea about any of this."

Omar nodded, a sad expression on his face. "I know, and I'm sorry you had to find out like this. But I needed to tell you. Mama has caused enough pain for our family, and I don't want her to continue hurting us...hurting you."

Nikki reached out and placed a hand on Omar's arm. "I understand, and I appreciate you being honest. I can't imagine what it must have been like for you and Junior, growing up with all of this hanging over your heads."

Omar shrugged. "We didn't know any difference. Mama told us that George had abandoned us, and we believed her. But after he died, I couldn't help but wonder. That's why I started coming around, to see for myself what kind of person you were."

Now, among all the noise and echo, Nikki realized that Omar was standing beside her, that *he* had been the man she had seen in her home, and that George was among them in spirit, and that right now, hard as it was to comprehend, *this man* was the only semblance of reality.

They sat in silence for a moment longer, lost in their thoughts. Nikki was still processing everything she had learned, but she felt a sense of peace knowing that George had been a good man, despite the lies and betrayal he had faced.

Nikki and Omar huddled in the darkness of the small room, trying to stay as quiet as possible. Nikki's heart was pounding in her chest, and she could hear Omar's breathing becoming more and more ragged.

"Omar, I have to get out of here," she whispered urgently. "Can you help me?"

Omar hesitated. "I don't know, Nikki. She's still my mother, and she's been through a lot."

"But this isn't right," Nikki said, her voice rising in frustration. "I'm trapped here, and she won't let me leave. Please, Omar. Do it for your father."

Suddenly, they heard footsteps coming down the hallway, and Nikki's heart skipped a beat. She could hear the voice on the other side of the door.

"Nikki. Are you okay in there?"

She took a deep breath and responded, "Yes, I'm okay."

Junior's voice followed, "If you're ready to apologize, I can let you out."

With a great splintering of wood, the door crashed open. Junior spun round, pointing a gun at the great figure that had just fallen aside. Nikki launched herself over the door to grab his arm, but Junior knocked her backwards with his elbow and she felt blood seep from a split lip.

"No – no, *don't!*"

Omar had stood up, lingering in the darkened landing, the face of his brother glaring at him.

"Nikki – Go! Now!"

Nikki didn't look back. She ran down the hallway and down the stairs as fast as she could. She could hear Mama's screams echoing behind her, but she pushed herself to run faster. She finally burst from the house, gasping for air.

CHAPTER SEVENTEEN.

N ikki's heart raced as she stumbled from the house of her abductors. She ran as fast as she could, her eyes scanning the darkened surroundings for any sign of help.

As she staggered, Nikki heard prolonged shouting coming from behind her. She didn't dare look back, afraid that Mama and Junior were coming after her.

Halfway along the road they'd left the dirty old car, abandoned to whoever wanted to deal with it. Nikki's fingers scrambled along the driver's side as best as they could, keeping herself low. The keys were gone, restraint and safety along with them.

She heard the screams only by accident, in brief pauses of heaving breath, each of them howling in bitterness and pain across the night like flaming javelins and burning to ashes before they could reach them.

Nikki clenched her fists and hit the car wildly, then screeched with pain as her bruised knuckles protested.

Slowly, the panic began to ebb, though her heart was still leaping erratically. At last, she removed her numb hands from clasping each other and widened her eyes, blinking in the nothingness. The dead of night was becoming so quiet.

Time froze. The darkness seemed to fold in upon her, crashing through her mind into a thought process unprepared for it, and shock kept her moving, one foot after the other, her fists still clenched tight and her mouth still slightly open, trying to understand what she was seeing.

Nikki's bare feet moved with resolute determination, her steps echoing against the pavement. She had escaped the confines of the house where she had been held captive, but the ghosts of her torment continued to haunt her mind. Hallucinations flickered at the edge of her vision, adding a chilling layer of uncertainty to her already fragile state.

Fear clung to her like a second skin, the realization of her vulnerability gnawing at her thoughts. The world around her seemed both vast and menacing, a labyrinth of shadows and hidden dangers. She shivered, her body aching from the remnants of captivity, but she refused to let despair claim her spirit.

As she walked, the enormity of her situation weighed upon her. Anything could happen to her now, the possibility of further harm lurking in every shadow. Yet a perverse notion took root within her troubled mind, that perhaps the worst had already transpired. Death, in its cold embrace, whispered a seductive promise of respite. But no, Nikki's survival instinct surged forth, demanding her perseverance.

Her fragmented thoughts coalesced into a single resolve: she had to make it home.

The concept of home, once a sanctuary of solace, had been tainted by the horrors she had endured. But in the depths of her being, a flickering ember of hope urged her forward. She had to reclaim her sense of self, to unravel the enigma of her captivity, and find meaning within the tangled web of her shattered existence.

The path ahead was treacherous, fraught with uncertainty and trepidation. Each step echoed with a mix of determination and apprehension, her senses attuned to the slightest movement or sound. The world seemed poised on a precipice, balanced between salvation and further anguish.

Yet through the haze of fear, Nikki found a reservoir of strength. She summoned it, drawing upon the flickering flame of resilience that burned within her. She would endure, for herself and for those whose stories had been silenced. The ghosts of her past would become the catalysts for her transformation, driving her toward a future where truth and justice could prevail.

With each step, Nikki carved a path through the darkness, determined to reclaim her life, and make sense of the unfathomable. The road ahead may be fraught with perils, but she refused to succumb. For she had tasted the bitter fruit of captivity, and from its depths, a fierce determination had blossomed.

PART THREE - PATH TO NEW BEGINNINGS

CHAPTER EIGHTEEN.

ONE MONTH LATER...
As she stepped into the gym, her radiant smile reached her eyes, exuding a newfound strength and resilience. The heavy cloak of grief that had weighed her down was gradually lifting, allowing her to move forward with a determination to reclaim the confident woman she once was.

Gone were the days of isolating herself from those around her. Nikki now found herself engaging in friendly conversations with the women she encountered at the gym. She no longer stood on the periphery, but instead, she embraced the camaraderie and support that surrounded her. Though she still guarded her innermost thoughts and feelings, she had taken small steps toward letting others in, recognizing that healing could be found in the warmth of connection.

As Nikki pushed herself through her workout routine, her mind drifted to the memories she carried within. The echoes of her ordeal occasionally surfaced, threatening to unravel her newfound strength. Yet, she had learned to block out intrusive thoughts, reminding herself of the progress she had made and the power she possessed. She refused to allow the scars of her past to define her future.

At home, Nikki sought solace in the tranquility of her sanctuary. With a cup of tea in hand, she settled into her favorite armchair, allowing her thoughts to wander. She acknowledged the trials she had faced, the pain that had once consumed her, but she also recognized the indomitable spirit that had guided her through the darkest of moments.

With a deep breath, Nikki repeated her mantra, a reminder to herself: "I am strong. I am resilient. I am in control of my own narrative." It was a constant affirmation, a gentle push to believe in her own worth and to never forget the strength she had found within herself.

Nikki sat in the comfortable armchair, facing her therapist. The soft glow of the room provided a soothing ambiance, creating a safe space for her to delve into the depths of her emotions. She took a deep breath, steadying herself as she prepared to share her innermost thoughts.

"I miss him," Nikki began, her voice tinged with a mixture of longing and sorrow. "George was my rock, my everything. Losing him has left a void in my life that I'm struggling to fill."

Her therapist leaned forward; his kind eyes filled with empathy. "Tell me more about George. What made him so special to you?"

A bittersweet smile graced Nikki's lips as she recalled the memories, she held dear. "He was my best friend. We were planning to travel the world together, to experience different cultures, and make unforgettable memories. George had this way of making even the most ordinary moments feel extraordinary. His laughter was infectious, and his love was unwavering."

As Nikki spoke, she felt a sense of relief washing over her. Opening up about her grief allowed her to honor the love she had shared with George, keeping his memory alive in her heart. She shared stories, both joyful and tearful, painting a vivid picture of the man who had brought so much light into her life.

Her therapist listened attentively, offering words of compassion and understanding. He encouraged her to embrace her emotions, reminding her that it was normal to feel the depth of her grief. Together, they explored strategies to navigate the waves of sadness and create a space for healing.

However, as Nikki spoke openly about her grief for George, she remained guarded about the dark chapters that had unfolded before his untimely death. The horrors inflicted upon her by Mama and Junior remained locked away, hidden from the prying eyes of the outside world.

Nikki understood the importance of seeking support, but she wasn't yet ready to confront the depths of her traumatic experiences. The wounds were still raw, and the memories too painful to unearth. She feared that unveiling the truth would unravel the progress she had made in rebuilding her life.

For now, Nikki chose to focus on the love and loss she had experienced, allowing herself to grieve and honor the beautiful connection she had shared with George. In the therapeutic space, she found solace and guidance, a steady hand to navigate the tumultuous seas of her emotions.

As the session ended, her therapist commended Nikki for her courage in sharing her journey of grief. He reminded her that healing was a gradual process, unique to each individual, and that she had taken a significant step toward reclaiming her life.

Leaving the therapist's office, Nikki felt a renewed sense of hope. While the shadows of her past still loomed, she was determined to forge ahead, embracing the memories of her beloved George, and allowing herself the space to heal. She understood that true healing would require confronting her demons in due time, but for now, she focused on the strength within her, taking one step at a time toward a brighter future.

The image of the door lingered in Nikki's mind, haunting her thoughts long after the events unfolded. It was the door she remembered—open, a subtle sign of impending doom that she couldn't ignore. It played in a loop in her mind as she recounted the walk back from the house, retracing each step with meticulous precision, even in the enveloping darkness.

The gravel beneath her feet crunched rhythmically as she traversed the path across the old town, the arch serving as a gateway to the unknown. A shortcut through the shadowed depths of the old gardens led her onward, her steps light on the dew-soaked, forbidden lawn. No "keep off the grass" signs were needed in that place; it had long been the domain of alphas and fellows, silently warning trespassers of the consequences they would face.

Her journey continued, passing by Western Oaks, navigating the path that skirted her block. Finally, she ascended four flights of worn stone steps, determined to reach the top where her house stood, at the end of the hallway opposite George's old room.

As Nikki approached her house, she noticed that the door, which had always been closed before, was now ajar. The realization struck her with a chilling force. She had left it open. It was the last thing she remembered, and she berated herself for not recognizing the warning signs.

Deep down, she suspected foul play. The pieces of the puzzle began to fit together, forming a picture of malevolence and betrayal that lay hidden beneath the surface of her seemingly ordinary life. But the events that transpired after that pivotal moment remained elusive to her, lost in the recesses of her memory. It was as if her brain had shut down, unable to retrieve the fragments of that night. No matter how much her sister Kayla probed and questioned, the actual recollection remained stubbornly out of reach.

Occasionally, in the depths of the night, Nikki would awaken with a vivid image etched in her mind. It was different from the grainy polaroids of the house they held her captive in, devoid of lighting and suffused with a menacing atmosphere. In this vision, the lamps in her own home emitted a dim glow, casting a subtle warmth upon her flushed cheeks—evidence of the remnants of life. She watched herself, a mere specter, running across the room, stumbling over a rug and falling to her knees beside George's waiting arms. Then, the piercing screams echoed through the air, reverberating in her ears.

Uncertainty clouded her understanding of this image. Was it a memory, a nightmare, or perhaps a twisted fusion of both? The truth remained elusive, teasing her from the periphery of her consciousness.

Yet, despite the lingering mysteries and unrelenting turmoil, Nikki found solace in one undeniable fact—she was home. The familiarity of her surroundings, the subtle embrace of the dimly lit lamps, served as a bittersweet reminder of the life she had left behind. It was a sanctuary, a refuge amidst the storm that raged within her.

But Nikki knew that the tranquility of home was merely a temporary respite. The answers she sought, the truth she yearned to uncover, lay shrouded in the shadows that loomed ahead. Determination burned within her, fueling her resolve to confront the darkness that had shattered her world. The journey ahead would be treacherous, fraught with danger and uncertainty, but she vowed to use her head and persevere, no matter what awaited her on the path of truth.

CHAPTER NINETEEN.

Nikki's heart pounded in her chest as she walked through the bustling town. The sounds of chatter and footsteps that usually blended into a comforting symphony now seemed to reverberate with an unsettling energy. The encounter with the girl had left her on edge, and her mind raced with questions, desperately seeking answers to the cryptic warning she had received.

She couldn't shake off the feeling of being watched, as if unseen eyes followed her every move. The once-familiar streets now felt unfamiliar and filled with a tinge of uncertainty. Nikki quickened her pace, the weight of the girl's words weighing heavily on her mind.

As she navigated through the crowd, she couldn't help but notice fleeting glimpses of familiar faces. Faces that she had hoped to leave behind, but now seemed to resurface with a haunting persistence. Were they mere figments of her imagination, or was there a deeper meaning behind their presence?

Doubt gnawed at Nikki's mind, and she found herself constantly looking over her shoulder, scanning the crowd for any signs of danger. The city, once a haven of vibrant energy, now felt like a labyrinth of shadows and hidden threats.

The sun began its descent, casting long shadows that stretched across the pavement. Nikki's anxiety deepened with the fading light, as if darkness itself held the answers she sought. With a determined resolve, she changed her direction, drawn to the enigmatic allure of the city's backstreets.

As she ventured further into the labyrinthine alleys, the atmosphere grew denser, suffused with an eerie silence that hung in the air. The familiar sounds of chatter and footsteps faded into distant echoes, replaced by an unsettling stillness that sent shivers down Nikki's spine.

Nikki's senses heightened, and every creak of a rusted gate or flutter of a distant curtain seemed magnified. She felt the weight of invisible eyes upon her, a presence that seemed to lurk just beyond her field of vision. Her breath quickened, and she could almost taste the air thick with apprehension.

In the dimly lit alley, Nikki caught a glimpse of movement—a shadowy figure darting behind a corner. Her heart skipped a beat, and adrenaline surged through her veins. Against her better judgment, she followed, her curiosity and a growing determination propelling her forward.

The narrow alley twisted and turned, a labyrinth of mystery and intrigue. Each step brought her deeper into the unknown, closer to the truth she yearned to uncover. Time seemed to stretch, as if the city held its breath, waiting for Nikki's next move.

Finally, she arrived at a secluded courtyard bathed in moonlight. The figure she had been pursuing stood at the center, backlit by the pale glow. It was the girl—the one who had issued the warning, the one who seemed to hold the key to the enigma that had consumed Nikki's thoughts.

Without a word, the girl turned to face Nikki, her eyes brimming with both fear and determination. Her voice, when she finally spoke, carried the weight of the unseen dangers that lurked in the shadows.

"You must understand," the girl began, her voice a whisper that cut through the silence. "There are forces at play, ones that cannot be ignored. They never forget, and they won't stop until they achieve what they desire."

Before Nikki could gather her thoughts to respond, the girl released her grip and swiftly turned away, blending back into the bustling crowd. Nikki stood there, her mind swirling with questions, her heart racing with a mix of confusion and apprehension.

The encounter left her rattled, her sense of security shattered once again. Who was this girl, and why did she feel compelled to issue such a warning? The intensity in her eyes spoke of shared secrets and a hidden world that Nikki had yet to comprehend.

Nikki tried to push the encounter to the back of her mind as she continued her walk, but the girl's words echoed persistently, haunting her thoughts. They carried an air of foreboding, as if an unseen danger lurked in the shadows, waiting for the opportune moment to strike.

Her steps became more cautious, her eyes scanning the surroundings with heightened vigilance. She couldn't shake off the feeling that she was being watched and that unseen eyes followed her every move. The once-familiar streets now held a tinge of uncertainty, as if the façade of normalcy had been peeled away to reveal a darker reality.

Nikki found herself in the bustling heart of the city, seeking solace in the anonymity and the hum of activity that surrounded her. The hotel she had chosen provided a temporary respite from the familiar walls of her home, offering a change of scenery and a chance to clear her mind. As she checked into her room, she reminded herself of the strength she had cultivated and the progress she had made in her healing journey.

The hotel room felt both foreign and comforting, a space that held the promise of escape from the ghosts that still lingered in her mind. The city lights twinkled outside the window, casting a soft glow on the streets below. Nikki took a moment to appreciate the vibrant energy that pulsed through the city, drawing strength from its vibrancy.

She knew that staying here for the night was not a permanent solution, but it was a necessary step in regaining her composure. The strange encounter with the girl and her cryptic warning had rattled her, reminding her that the shadows of the past could resurface at any moment. But Nikki was determined not to let fear dictate her actions or unravel the progress she had made.

In the solitude of the hotel room, Nikki made a conscious effort to ground herself.

She closed her eyes, took deep breaths, and focused on the present moment. She repeated affirmations to herself, reminding herself of her resilience and the strength that resided within her.

As she delved deeper into her meditation, memories and emotions began to resurface, demanding her attention. The image of Junior's menacing face flashed through her mind, and the weight of Mama's betrayal weighed heavy on her heart. The truth about Omar, George, and their tangled web of secrets became a tangled knot within her thoughts.

Nikki opened her eyes, realizing that finding solace and healing wouldn't be as simple as a change of scenery. It would take time—time to process the trauma she had endured, time to unravel the complex emotions that still bound her. She understood that her healing journey was a gradual process, one that required patience and self-compassion.

CHAPTER TWENTY.

Coming home, Nikki stood frozen on her doorstep, her heart pounding in her chest as she stared at Omar, a mix of shock and apprehension washing over her. The sight of him there, unannounced, and unexpected, sent a wave of confusion through her already tumultuous mind. She couldn't understand why he had come, why he had disrupted the fragile equilibrium she had managed to rebuild.

"Omar," she managed to say, her voice trembling with a mixture of anger and fear. "What are you doing here? I told you to stay away. I've put everything behind me, and I haven't even gone to the police. You need to leave."

Omar's expression softened, his eyes reflecting a hint of regret. "Nikki, I shouldn't be here, but I had to see you. There's something you need to know. They're angry, and they're coming. You need to be prepared."

His words sent a chill down Nikki's spine, the gravity of his warning sinking in. The mention of anger and impending danger reignited her sense of vulnerability, the fear she had fought so hard to keep at bay threatening to consume her once again.

She took a step back, distancing herself from Omar. "I don't know what you're talking about," she said, her voice laced with uncertainty. "I can't handle this. I can't go back to that place. Please, just leave."

Omar's gaze held a mixture of sympathy and urgency. He seemed torn, caught between his concern for Nikki's safety and the weight of his own burdens. "Nikki, I understand your fear, but you can't ignore this. We need to confront the truth together, to protect ourselves. I'm sorry for bringing this into your life, but we can't turn a blind eye to what's coming."

A surge of emotions coursed through Nikki's veins, her mind spinning with the choices before her. She had worked so hard to move forward, to find a semblance of peace amidst the chaos that had defined her existence. The idea of delving back into the darkness, of confronting the threats she had tried so desperately to forget, filled her with dread.

With a heavy sigh, she shook her head. "I can't, Omar. I won't let myself be dragged back into that world. I've made a choice to put it all behind me, to rebuild my life. I can't jeopardize that."

Omar's face fell, disappointment etched across his features. He knew that convincing Nikki to face the truth would be an uphill battle. He respected her decision but couldn't shake the concern that gnawed at him.

"I understand," he said quietly, his voice tinged with resignation. "Just remember, Nikki, I'll be there if you ever need me. Stay safe. And there's something else... something you should know."

"What is it?"

"It's your sister... Kayla... she... she knew!"

With those final words, Omar turned and walked away, leaving Nikki standing on her doorstep, her heart heavy with conflicting emotions. As she closed the door behind her, she couldn't shake the feeling of unease that lingered in the air. The encounter had rattled her, casting doubts on the peace she had fought so hard to reclaim. She knew that she would need to confront her past eventually, but for now, she had chosen to keep it buried, hoping against hope that it would remain there, locked away in the depths of her memory.

Nikki sat alone in her dimly lit living room, the weight of the recent encounter still lingering in the air. Fear coiled in the pit of her stomach, threatening to consume her, but she refused to let it overpower her resolve. She had fought too hard to rebuild her life, to reclaim her sense of security and strength, and she was determined not to let anyone, or anything ruin it again.

Drawing in a deep breath, Nikki reminded herself of the progress she had made. She had taken steps forward, slowly but surely, embracing her own resilience and refusing to be defined by the traumas of her past. The memory of her husband George and the love they shared remained a bittersweet ache within her, but she had learned to carry it with grace, to honor his memory while forging a new path for herself.

As she sat there in the stillness, she allowed herself to acknowledge the fear that coursed through her veins. It was a natural response, a reminder of the vulnerability that came with being a survivor. But she refused to let that fear paralyze her, to let it dictate her choices or unravel the progress she had made.

In the face of uncertainty, Nikki found strength in her own resilience. She had discovered an inner fortitude she never knew existed, a fire that burned brightly within her. It was a flame fueled by determination, by the refusal to let her past define her future.

She had learned to trust herself, to listen to the whispers of her intuition that guided her away from danger. And while the encounter with Omar had shaken her, she knew deep down that she had made the right choice in distancing herself from the turmoil of her past. It was a choice she made out of self-preservation, out of a fierce desire to protect the life she had worked so hard to rebuild.

As the night wore on, Nikki resolved to strengthen her defenses, both physical and emotional. She reinforced the locks on her doors, ensuring her home remained a sanctuary of safety. She immersed herself in self-defense classes, honing her skills and empowering herself with the knowledge that she could protect herself if the need arose.

But beyond the physical precautions, Nikki focused on fortifying her mental and emotional resilience. She sought solace in therapy, allowing herself to unravel the layers of grief and trauma that still lingered within her. Through the guidance of her therapist, she explored coping mechanisms and strategies to navigate the challenges that lay ahead.

In the quiet solitude of her home, Nikki made a promise to herself. She would not allow fear to dictate her choices. She would not let the ghosts of her past haunt her present. She would continue to fight for the life she deserved, one filled with joy, love, and freedom.

As the night drew to a close, Nikki found solace in the flickering flame of a candle, a symbol of the resilience that burned within her. With each passing moment, she became more determined, more resolute in her pursuit of a future that was hers alone to shape. And with every breath she took, she reclaimed her power, embracing the strength that would carry her forward into the unknown, ready to face whatever challenges may come her way.

CHAPTER TWENTY-ONE.

Nikki's heart pounded once more as she answered the door, greeted by the concerned face of her sister, Kayla. Her disappearance had caused worry and turmoil within their fractured relationship, a tangible strain that hung heavily in the air. Kayla stepped inside the house, her eyes scanning the disheveled state of her sister, a silent testament to the turmoil she had endured.

Without a word, Kayla set about caring for Nikki, her actions imbued with a tenderness that spoke volumes. She straightened Nikki's rumpled clothing, brushed a stray lock of hair away from her face, and enveloped her in a comforting embrace. It was a wordless exchange, an unspoken acknowledgment of their unbreakable bond as sisters.

For a time, Nikki remained silent, allowing Kayla's presence and gentle ministrations to envelop her. The weight of her recent experiences threatened to suffocate her, and she yearned for the solace of her sister's understanding. But as the minutes ticked by, a restlessness began to stir within Nikki, an urgent need to break the silence that had shrouded their relationship for far too long.

Finally, unable to contain the overwhelming truth any longer, Nikki's voice quivered as she blurted out the words that had consumed her thoughts. "I know, Kayla. I know that you knew about George and his second family."

A flicker of surprise and guilt crossed Kayla's features, her eyes widening momentarily before she composed herself. The truth, it seemed, had been unleashed, Pandora's box of secrets threatening to engulf their fragile connection.

Kayla took a step back, her gaze locked with Nikki's, the weight of unspoken truths hanging heavy in the air. For a moment, the sisters stood in a fragile standoff, the years of deception and unspoken words echoing through the space between them.

Finally, Kayla's voice broke the silence, her words laced with a mixture of sorrow and regret. "Nikki, I never meant for you to find out like this. I thought I was protecting you, shielding you from the pain and betrayal."

Nikki's eyes brimmed with a mixture of anger and hurt; her voice laced with a palpable anguish. "Protecting me? By keeping the truth hidden. How could you, Kayla? How could you let me live in ignorance while George led a double life?"

Tears welled in Kayla's eyes, mirroring the pain etched upon Nikki's face. "I know I made a terrible mistake, Nikki. I was afraid of the consequences; of the pain it would cause. But I see now that my silence only prolonged your suffering."

The room filled with the weight of their shared sorrow, the revelation of betrayal cutting through the frayed remnants of their once unbreakable bond. But beneath the pain, a flicker of understanding sparked between them—a realization that they were both victims of circumstances beyond their control.

Nikki's voice, though tinged with bitterness, held a hint of vulnerability. "Tell me everything, Kayla. I need to know the truth. Spare no details, no matter how painful. I deserve to hear it all."

And so, in that quiet room, the walls bore witness to a painful unraveling—a tapestry of secrets unfurled, exposing the hidden depths of George's deception. As Kayla recounted the story of George's second family, each word falling heavy upon Nikki's wounded heart, a newfound resolve took root within her.

Nikki knew perfectly well that she needed to deliver the coup de grace. Kayla's words had increased her sense of urgency. She had not yet found the right questions, but she knew it was the truth. Yet here she sat on the sofa, working things out in her head rather than dealing with the revelation that threatened to engulf the whole house, pressing against the walls, keeping the atmosphere continually stiff with tension. News anchors were babbling on the TV screen about the decorations in the Harbor Court Parade. Famous guests snaked towards the entrance and Nikki half listened as she noted down the things she was being told, the lies she was discovering.

In a different mood – a different life – Nikki might have found a way to stay calm and distract herself. But tonight, was not the night.

"How could you keep something like this from me?" Nikki yells, turning to face her sister. "This is something I deserved to know! The pain he…"

"I promised George that I wouldn't tell you," Kayla responds, her voice barely above a whisper. "He was ashamed, Nikki. He didn't want anyone to know what had happened to him."

"But this was my life, Kayla!" Nikki exclaims. "I had a right to know the truth about my husband, and you should have told me!"

"I know, I know," Kayla says, tears streaming down her face. "But I didn't want to hurt you. I thought I was doing the right thing by keeping his secret."

"You weren't," Nikki snaps back. "You were keeping me in the dark, and I can't forgive you for that."

Kayla looks at her sister, a look of hurt and regret on her face. "Sis, please," she says. "I know I messed up, and I'll never forgive myself for it."

Nikki takes a deep breath, trying to calm herself down. "Just leave," she says, her voice barely above a whisper. "I need some time alone."

Kayla nods, tears still streaming down her face. "I understand," she says softly. "But know that I love you, Nikki. And I'm here for you if you need me."

With that, Kayla left the house, and Nikki was left alone with her thoughts. She felt betrayed and hurt by her sister, but deep down, she knew that Kayla had only been trying to protect her. There was a knot in her stomach, a conflict, and an anger boiling over inside of her.

Nikki stood in the middle of the room, breathing heavily. Her hands were shaking, and tears were streaming down her face. She couldn't quite understand everything that had happened. The betrayal, the secrets, the danger. It was too much for her to handle.

She looked around the room, her eyes focusing on a vase sitting on the coffee table. In a fit of rage, she picked it up and threw it against the wall. Shattered ceramic littered the carpet. She took hold of a picture frame on the mantle, and threw it to the ground, watching as the glass broke into a thousand small pieces.

As she continued her rampage, a sudden sense of exhaustion overcame her. She fell to the ground, her body wracked with sobs. She couldn't keep it all in anymore.

The pain, the anger, the fear, the loss...

Quite suddenly, the lights flickered and burst out of existence, while the room was plunged into darkness. Nikki froze, her heart racing. She could hear scratches and banging sounds coming from outside. She tried to call out, but the terrible ideas in her imagination caught in her throat.

She stumbled through the dark, her arms outstretched, trying to find her way to the kitchen. She bumped into sharpness and shrieked in pain. Hyper aware now, she maintained her course in case someone was looking in on her through the window, intending to find her way among the shadows where she could gather a source of light.

Whatever she stumbled upon was part of the kitchen, and she felt her way through the drawers until she finally found the torch.

The scratching and banging sounds had grown louder, and Nikki could feel her fear rising. She made her way back to the living room, the beam of the torch illuminating her path. She couldn't see anything outside, but the sounds were getting closer.

She called out again, her voice shaking. Suddenly, the lights jolted back to life, and Nikki was blinded by the sudden brightness, dropping the torch in haste. She rubbed her eyes and looked around the room. She was *alone*. The scratching and banging sounds had stopped.

Nikki took a deep breath and steadied herself. She knew that she couldn't let fear and anger consume her. She needed to be strong, for herself and for George's memory. She kicked the torch away and sat down on the couch, her mind racing with all sorts of terrors.

The doorbell seemed to be half-ring. No one ever used it anyway, so it had to have been just a malfunction. But then, someone knocked sharply on the door with the sound of heavy knuckles. An explosion of furious barking told her that someone outside had set the neighbor's dog off. Then she thought she heard a woman's voice, angry but someone ineffectual:

"She knows. She knows it's me."

CHAPTER TWENTY-TWO.

Nikki stood at the threshold, peering into the darkness beyond her doorstep. The streetlights cast an eerie glow, illuminating empty sidewalks and silent houses. Confusion clouded her mind as she glanced left and right, searching for any sign of the person who had rung her doorbell. But there was no one in sight.

Puzzled, Nikki shrugged off the strange incident, chalking it up to her imagination by playing tricks on her. She closed the door, allowing the sense of unease to dissipate as she returned to the comfort of her home. However, the night soon took on a sinister tone, wrapping her surroundings in unsettling silence.

As Nikki moved through her house, the usual creaks and groans seemed amplified, echoing through the empty rooms. Every flicker of shadow caught her attention, making her heart skip a beat. Paranoia gnawed at her, whispering that someone was lurking, hiding just beyond her sight.

She tried to dismiss her fears, attributing the noises to the settling of an old house or the gusts of wind that swept through the neighborhood. Yet, the lingering unease refused to dissipate. Each fleeting shadow became a potential threat, every sound a whisper of hidden danger.

Nikki's senses sharpened, her mind playing tricks on her with every passing moment. The ticking of the clock became a countdown, a reminder of the passing time and her mounting anxiety. She double-checked the locks on the doors and windows, ensuring that her sanctuary remained secure. But still, the feeling of being watched persisted, an unseen presence lingering in the corners of her perception.

She sought solace in her rationality, attempting to dispel the growing unease. But as the night wore on, the boundary between reality and imagination blurred. Shadows danced in her peripheral vision, teasing her with their fleeting movements. She swore she heard whispers carried on the wind, unintelligible voices that sent shivers down her spine.

Nikki's phone buzzed, startling her. She fumbled to retrieve it from her pocket, her hands trembling with trepidation. A text message illuminated the screen, from Kayla: "I see you."

*

Nikki's heart raced as she heard the urgent knock at the door. Hope surged within her, thinking it might be Kayla, seeking refuge after the unsettling text message. Filled with a mixture of anticipation and trepidation, she swung the door open, only to be confronted by an unexpected sight—Junior and Mama standing on her doorstep.

Shock and disbelief coursed through Nikki's veins as she stared at the two individuals who had caused her so much torment. Without hesitation, she slammed the door shut, her hands trembling as she scrambled to slide the bolt across, desperately securing the barrier between herself and her assailants.

The resounding thud against the door sent shivers down her spine. Junior and Mama were banging on the door with an intensity that hinted at their determination to gain entry. Fear gripped Nikki's chest, her mind racing for a solution.

"Get out of here!" she shouted, her voice filled with a mixture of anger and terror.

"Leave me alone!"

But their response was far from what she hoped for. Their voices rose in unison, their words dripping with malevolence. "We have unfinished business, Nikki. We won't let you escape."

Frantically, Nikki searched for a means to defend herself. Her eyes fell upon the baseball bat tucked away in the corner of the living room. With a surge of adrenaline, she darted toward it, her footsteps echoing through the house.

But before she could reach her makeshift weapon, a bone-chilling crash reverberated from downstairs. The sound of shattering glass echoed through the silence, confirming her worst fears. Mama had obtained her own bat, and she was ruthlessly smashing in the windows, splintering the sanctuary Nikki had tried to create.

Panic set in as the realization dawned on her—time was running out. She had to act swiftly, decisively. With determination fueling her movements, Nikki sprinted back toward the staircase, her heart pounding in her chest.

As she reached the top step, a deafening slam echoed through the house. Junior had forced his way through the front door, shattering it with his brute strength. Nikki turned her head, her eyes widening in horror as she saw him standing before her, a menacing figure ready to strike.

Without hesitation, Junior lunged at Nikki, his rage propelling him forward. She barely had time to react before she was knocked to the ground, the impact stealing her breath away. Pain radiated through her body as she hit the floor, disoriented and vulnerable.

Struggling to regain her composure, Nikki fought against the overwhelming darkness that threatened to consume her. She knew she couldn't give in, couldn't surrender to the mercy of her assailants. With every ounce of strength, she could muster, she pushed herself up, her eyes locked on Junior's looming figure.

Nikki's world spiraled into darkness as the cold grip of dread tightened around her. The realization washed over her like a frigid wave—she was held captive at gunpoint, at the mercy of Junior and Mama's twisted agenda. Their heavy footsteps reverberated through the house, punctuated by a cacophony of chaos. Each sound was an eerie echo, carrying a weight of impending danger, until finally, they forced her up the stairs, shrouding her from view.

Fear coiled in Nikki's gut, a desperate plea for time, for an opportunity to escape the clutches of her captors. She mustered the courage to speak, her voice laced with a fragile hope. "What are you going to do?" she asked, her words quivering in the air.

Mama and Junior exchanged a sinister glance, their eyes gleaming with a twisted sense of purpose. Mama's voice dripped with venom as she replied, her words laden with resentment and bitterness. "I told you! You're going to pay for George's mistakes," she spat. "He abandoned us, and now we're going to make you pay for it."

Nikki's heart sank, the weight of their accusations pressing upon her weary soul. She tried to summon the strength to deny their claims, to convince them of her innocence, but her words faltered in her throat. The truth had become a burden she couldn't escape—the knowledge that she had unknowingly been a part of George's hidden life, a pawn in his deceit.

Desperation clawed at Nikki's thoughts as she attempted to bluff her way out, to claim ignorance of George's misdeeds. But the cold gaze of her captors dismissed her feeble attempts at deception. Junior's voice dripped with menace as he spoke, his words sending chills down her spine. "You're lying," he sneered. "You had to have known something. You were his wife, weren't you?"

A deep sadness settled over Nikki, her head bowing in reluctant acceptance of their accusation. She had loved George with unwavering devotion, and now she faced the consequences of his betrayal, both real and perceived. The weight of guilt threatened to crush her spirit, but she refused to let it extinguish the flicker of determination within her.

Nikki's trembling hand clasped her wedding ring, the symbol of a love she had believed to be pure. She couldn't bear the thought of losing her life, of succumbing to the consequences of another's sins. But Mama and Junior were unrelenting in their pursuit of vengeance, their hearts devoid of mercy. There seemed to be no way out, no escape from the clutches of their twisted vendetta.

Just as hope threatened to slip away, their words struck with a chilling finality. "You will die tonight," Mama declared, her voice devoid of emotion, as if discussing the most mundane of topics. "And then, we'll go find your sister, Kayla."

The revelation pierced Nikki's heart like a knife. The safety and well-being of her sister, Kayla, now hung in the balance, at the mercy of the same forces that sought to extinguish Nikki's life. Panic surged through her veins, mingling with the resolve that burned deep within her.

In the face of imminent danger, Nikki's mind raced, desperately seeking a glimmer of hope, a plan for escape. But her thoughts were shrouded in darkness, her mind unable to grasp a viable solution. The weight of her own mortality pressed upon her, and the fate of her sister hung precariously in the balance.

Nikki's eyes blazed with anger, her voice quivering as she confronted Mama and Junior. Their accusations, their threats against Kayla, ignited a fire within her. She couldn't fathom the depths of their twisted reasoning.

"What the hell are you talking about?" she shouted, her voice laced with fury. "Why Kayla?"

Mama's face remained impassive, devoid of emotion, as she met Nikki's gaze. Her voice held a haunting calmness as she spoke, each word landing with a chilling weight. "Because she's a part of you, Nikki," she said, her tone softened. "And no one will ever find out what happened to either of you."

Nikki's heart plummeted, a mix of fear and despair coursing through her veins. She had been so certain of their intent, so convinced that Mama and Junior posed a genuine threat to her beloved sister. But in that moment, a flicker of doubt stirred within her—a question of whether their claims were rooted in a distorted reality.

Mama seemed disinterested in further probing Nikki for information about George's hidden life. Junior, on the other hand, had resigned himself to George's absence, accepting that he had faded from their lives. Mama's offhand comment about her impending loss piqued Nikki's curiosity, her confusion unraveling in a torrent of questions.

"What do you mean, with him soon enough?" Nikki asked, her anger giving way to a sense of bewilderment.

Mama's gaze softened, tinged with sadness. She regarded Nikki with a mix of regret and resignation. "We're not long for this world, Nikki," she revealed, her voice tinged with a whisper. "I have cancer, and Junior... Well, he's a fighter. But he knows this world won't ever take him alive. We have little time left, and you're going first."

Shock rippled through Nikki's being. The revelation of Mama's illness shattered the facade of unyielding hostility, replacing it with a fragile vulnerability. She hadn't known the depths of Mama's suffering, the burden she carried within her. A sense of empathy washed over Nikki, a realization that despite the pain they had inflicted upon her, they too were facing their own battles.

"I'm sorry," Nikki murmured softly, her voice tinged with remorse. "I had no idea."

Mama's touch was gentle as she patted Nikki's hand, her eyes clouded with sadness. "It's alright," she said, her voice filled with a mixture of resignation and regret. "We don't have much time left in this world, but we wanted to make things right before we go. We're sorry we have to do this, but you need to pay for your mistakes."

Nikki's emotions swirled within her, a turbulent mix of anger, sympathy, and a glimmer of understanding. She despised Mama and Junior for the torment they had inflicted upon her, for the relentless pursuit of vengeance. Yet, the weight of their impending mortality tugged at her heartstrings, urging her to find a resolution in the face of their twisted intentions.

"I'm sorry too," Nikki whispered, her voice filled with a profound sadness. "But you need to find peace, to let go of this darkness before it's too late. Do you understand?"

Mama's gaze held a touch of sorrow, a flicker of regret dancing within her eyes. "I'm sorry, Nikki," she murmured, her voice laden with genuine remorse. "But this is how it has to be. We'll tell Kayla you said goodbye."

Junior's grip tightened around the gun; his intentions resolute.

CHAPTER TWENTY-THREE.

Nikki stood frozen on the staircase, her senses overwhelmed by a whirlwind of perplexing images and fragmented memories. Each passing thought flickered with disconcerting speed, leaving her grappling to make sense of the chaos that consumed her mind. Amidst the cacophony, a somber refrain echoed within her, a voice laden with regret and despair. "It wasn't meant to be like this. It wasn't meant to be this way."

Within the labyrinth of her thoughts, a flicker of someone else's first thought found its place, like a shard of distant wisdom embedded in her consciousness. George's voice emerged, his words piercing through the haze of confusion. "Use your head... no matter what," he had once counseled her.

As the weight of his advice settled upon her, Nikki's resolve solidified. Lowering her head, she channeled an unexpected surge of determination, akin to a seasoned flanker charging forward on the field of battle. The force of her motion propelled her towards Mama, a figure much larger than her own, and with a swift and resolute strike, she sent the woman tumbling aside, a mere puppet in her path. Mama flailed and fought against the sudden assault, her body hurtling down the stairs, her descent painting a picture of chaos and disarray. Junior, consumed by a furious rage, followed closely in pursuit, his anguished screams echoing through the air.

"Get up, Mama! Get up!" his voice reverberated with desperate urgency.

The sight that greeted Nikki as she approached the motionless figure of Mama lying slumped across the floor of the hallway gripped her heart with indescribable anguish. Blood seeped from beneath Mama's head, mingling with the wounds on her hands, evidence of the violence that had unfolded. Yet, it was the lifeless gaze emanating from her open eyes that haunted Nikki most profoundly. In that chilling stillness, the weight of irrevocable loss settled upon her shoulders, an unwelcome burden she could not ignore.

Time stood suspended in that harrowing moment, as Nikki's mind raced to comprehend the enormity of the situation. The remnants of her fragmented memories danced before her eyes, weaving an intricate tapestry of shattered lives and broken promises. The threads of their interconnected past began to unravel, revealing a darker truth that had lurked just beneath the surface.

Driven by a mixture of fear, urgency, and an unyielding determination to uncover the truth, Nikki descended the stairs in a frantic rush. She bypassed Junior, her focus fixated solely upon the lifeless form that lay before her. As she knelt by Mama's side, her hands trembling with a mix of trepidation and grief, a profound sense of finality settled over her.

Mama had slipped away, forever lost to the world, leaving behind unanswered questions and shattered remnants of a once-intertwined existence. In that moment, Nikki felt the weight of her responsibility grow exponentially. She knew she couldn't turn back now, couldn't shy away from the unsettling path that lay before her.

Drawing a shuddering breath, she closed her eyes briefly, steeling herself for the arduous journey ahead. The road to truth would be fraught with danger, obscured by shadows, but she vowed to use her head, to confront the darkness that had enveloped their lives, no matter what.

SECONDS PASSED... flashes spun and whirled...

Time was motionless...

It stood still.

It passed through a thousand single tragedies. No, it was only a minute or so...

Two people were standing looking down on a dead woman...

Slowly, very slowly, Nikki and Junior lifted their heads and looked into each other's eyes.

*

Junior laughed.

He said, "So that's it, is it, Nikki?"

Nikki said, "There's no-one here now except the two of us." Her voice was little more than a whisper.

Junior said, "Exactly. So, we know where we stand, right?" Nikki nodded.

Junior shrugged his shoulders.

Their eyes met again.

Nikki thought:

"Why did I never see his face properly before? A wolf – That's what it is - a wolf's face... Those horrible features."

Junior said, with a dangerous snarl in his voice:

"This is the end, you know. We've come to the truth now. And it's the end."

Nikki said quietly: "I understand..."

She stared out into the darkness. She had stared into the dark maybe once too often. As late as yesterday? Or was it the day before?

He had said those words - those exact words. "This is the end."

He said with an acceptance - almost with welcome.

But to Nikki the words, the thought, brought rebellion. No, it should not be the end.

She looked down again and crouched at the dead woman's side.

She said, "Poor Mama."

Junior sneered. He said, "What's this? Feminist pity?"

Nikki replied: "Why not? Haven't you any?" He said, "I've got no pity for you! Don't expect it!" His tone warned her.

She jumped to her feet and let out a painful moan. The noise was such that Nikki closed her eyes for a second and did not see Junior move across the room. He had moved a yard or two away and was facing her, revolver in hand.

"So, this was the end game, was it?"

He shrugged. He held it steadily and unwaveringly.

Death was very near to Nikki Lewis now. It had, she knew, never been nearer. So close, in fact, that she could almost feel George beside her…

"Give me the gun, brother."

She felt a thrill of shock. She didn't need to ask who was standing there, holding her hand. She already knew. She squeezed Omar's hand a little tighter.

Junior laughed.

Omar said,

"Come on, it's over."

Nikki watched them both. Her quick brain was working. Which way - which method talk them over - lulls him into a false sense of security - or a swift dash.

Not often enough in her life, Nikki had taken the less risky way. She took it now.

Junior spoke slowly. Authoritatively.

"Now look, brother, just listen – "

A rustle, the blur of a large hand, and Omar lunged. Quick as a wolf - as any vicious, lumbering creature… The gunpoint grazed his chest as he slammed Junior sideways; the brothers fell to the ground, rolled over and attacked again, and this time Junior fell backwards in his stride, with Omar on top of him, trapped between the wall and the couch. Omar had one of Junior's wrists, but he couldn't see where the gun was: all was darkness, and he threw a punch that hit Junior hard under the chin, knocking his head back and sending him flying; Junior punched again, and Omar hit the wall; he tried to sit up, with his brother's lower body pinning his right arm to the ground, and the gun struck him hard in the temple: he felt it; the flow of warm blood, and the white-hot stinging pain.

Nikki's shaking body stayed poised in mid-spring, edging away from the two men brawling like wild animals. She watched as they crashed heavily into the ground.

Junior and Omar both came bounding into the hallway. Nikki fled towards the door, unable to calm her adrenaline and confusion that she could, at last, escape.

"Nikki! Go!" Omar screamed.

She staggered into the blistering night, past the bells, ignoring the red-hot jabs of the cuts in her feet, moving awkwardly to steady herself, not daring to look back.

But there was no need for caution. Not anymore.

A single shot rang out in the dead of night.

Chapter Twenty-Four.

NINE HOURS LATER:

Within the bustling heart of downtown Washington, amidst the relentless ebb and flow of hurried pedestrians, a young couple's steps faltered as their searching gazes settled upon a sight both disconcerting and enigmatic. Before them stood a woman, disheveled and barefoot, her presence seemingly trapped within the confines of her own mind. Concern etched deeply upon their faces, they approached her cautiously, drawn by a mixture of worry and curiosity.

"Excuse me, miss," the young woman ventured, her voice carrying a delicate blend of empathy and intrigue. "Are you alright?"

No response escaped the woman's lips, her vacant stare fixed upon a distant horizon that only she could discern. Yet within the labyrinth of her thoughts, a vivid tableau unfolded, a vision so vivid it consumed her very being. In her mind's eye, she found herself transported to a sterile white room, George's presence beside her. Their hands intertwined, tears streaming down her anguished face, a palpable sorrow enveloping them both. But amidst the haze, his gentle voice permeated the air, bidding her a heartbreaking farewell.

"I have to go," his words whispered softly, his figure slowly receding into the embrace of luminous ethereal light.

In the blink of an eye, Nikki's consciousness snapped back to the present, leaving her disoriented and vulnerable, a fleeting sense of disconnect lingering in the air. She blinked, her surroundings abruptly coming into sharp focus, the concerned couple still awaiting a glimpse of comprehension from her troubled countenance.

Gradually regaining a semblance of composure, Nikki's eyes welled with unshed tears, her voice trembling as she mustered an explanation. "I... I'm sorry," she managed to utter, her words laced with sorrow and confusion. "I don't know what happened."

The young couple exchanged glances, their worry deepening at the depths of her distress. Extending a comforting hand, they guided her gently to a nearby bench, offering solace in their compassionate presence. As she sat, her mind teetered on the precipice of that vivid encounter, grappling with the blurred boundaries between reality and the ethereal.

Though shaken to her core, Nikki felt a flicker of gratitude for the kindness bestowed upon her by the compassionate couple. With a valiant effort, she mustered a weak smile, concealing the inner turmoil that threatened to engulf her very soul.

In a hushed voice, barely audible, she whispered a cryptic phrase, as if invoking an unknown force. "I have to go."

Nikki boarded the subway, seeking solace in the anonymity of the bustling city. As the train rattled along its tracks, she gazed out the window, watching the urban landscape whiz by. The noise and chaos of the city gradually faded into the background, replaced by a sense of tranquility as she neared her destination—the harbor.

Stepping off the subway, Nikki followed the familiar path that led her to the boardwalk. The salty breeze kissed her cheeks, carrying with it a soothing scent of the sea. The sounds of seagulls echoed in the air, their cries blending harmoniously with the lapping of the waves against the shore.

Finding a quiet spot on the boardwalk, Nikki stood alone, embracing the solitude that enveloped her. The vast expanse of the water stretched out before her, a mirror reflecting the shimmering sunlight. The rhythmic ebb and flow of the tide provided a soothing backdrop to her thoughts.

For the first time in what felt like an eternity, Nikki was truly alone. No distractions, no judgments, just the serenity of the harbor and her own introspection. She closed her eyes, allowing the gentle breeze to caress her face as if it carried away the burdens that had weighed heavily on her heart.

In the stillness of that moment, Nikki contemplated her journey—both the tangible one she had taken to reach this harbor and the intangible one she had embarked upon since George's passing. The chaos and confusion that had consumed her mind gradually faded, replaced by a sense of clarity, and understanding.

She realized that amidst the turbulence and uncertainties of life, it was essential to find moments of solitude, to retreat to a place where she could unravel her thoughts and emotions. Here, on the boardwalk, she could let go of the masks she wore and be her authentic self.

As she opened her eyes, a renewed sense of strength coursed through her veins. The vastness of the ocean before her reminded her of the vastness within herself—a depth of resilience and resilience she had yet to fully explore.

Nikki's mind wandered, seeking solace amidst the chaos that had engulfed her existence. She contemplated the enigmatic nature of life and death, grappling with questions that had haunted humanity since time immemorial. Her gaze drifted towards the window, where a flock of birds soared through the sky, their graceful wings slicing through the air.

The world outside seemed both distant and intimately connected to her inner musings. The birds, oblivious to the turmoil in her heart, gilded effortlessly, their synchronized movements hinting at a deeper harmony in the universe.

During her contemplation, Nikki found herself fixating on the concept of energy. She pondered the ebb and flow of life, the intricate dance between existence and transcendence. If energy can neither be created nor destroyed, she reasoned, then what becomes of it when our earthly vessels cease to function?

The fog, the smoke, the haze—all symbols of impermanence and transition—flitted through her thoughts. Like tendrils of mist dissipating in the morning sun, human life too must undergo a metamorphosis. And yet, Nikki couldn't shake the belief that the essence of who we are, the energy that courses through our beings, must find its place in the grand tapestry of existence.

In the late afternoon, Nikki found herself sitting in the cozy office of her therapist, Dr. Thompson. The soft light filtering through the curtains created a warm and inviting atmosphere, putting her somewhat at ease. She had made the decision to seek professional help, recognizing the importance of sharing her experiences and the weight they carried.

Dr. Thompson sat across from Nikki, her kind eyes filled with genuine concern and empathy. Nikki took a deep breath, her fingers nervously fidgeting with the edge of her sweater. It was time to open up, but she knew that she had to be careful about how much she revealed.

"I've been having these dreams lately," Nikki began tentatively, choosing her words carefully. "They're quite vivid and unsettling. They feel so real, you know?"

Dr. Thompson nodded, encouraging her to continue. "Dreams can often provide insights into our subconscious mind," she said gently. "What have these dreams been about?"

Nikki glanced around the room, ensuring that they were indeed alone. Satisfied with the privacy, she leaned in closer to Dr. Thompson, her voice barely above a whisper. "They're... they're about a past relationship, a difficult one," Nikki confessed, her eyes welling up with unshed tears. "I see flashes of memories, moments that I thought were long buried. It's as if my mind is trying to process something that I've been avoiding."

Dr. Thompson leaned forward, her demeanor compassionate and non-judgmental. "It's understandable to have such dreams when there are unresolved emotions from the past," she said softly. "Sometimes our subconscious mind finds ways to bring those emotions to the surface, even if we've buried them deep within ourselves."

Nikki nodded, feeling a sense of relief at being able to discuss these dreams without revealing their true origin. She knew that it was necessary to protect herself and those she cared about from the unsettling truth.

"I've been trying to make sense of these dreams," Nikki continued, her voice steady.

"But it's been a struggle. They leave me feeling unsettled, haunted even."

Dr. Thompson reached out and placed a comforting hand on Nikki's arm. "It takes time to process difficult emotions and experiences," she reassured her. "It's important to give yourself permission to feel and to heal at your own pace. Remember, you don't have to face this journey alone."

Nikki nodded, appreciating the support and understanding she found in Dr. Thompson's words. She knew that she had made the right decision in seeking therapy, allowing herself a safe space to share her burden while maintaining a necessary level of privacy.

As the session drew to a close, Nikki felt a sense of contentment wash over her. She had taken the first step towards healing, acknowledging the impact of her past experiences, even if she couldn't reveal the full truth. She understood that her therapy sessions would be a valuable tool for self-reflection and growth, helping her navigate the complexities of her emotions.

Chapter Twenty-Five.

Nikki walked into the excessively busy coffee shop, the aroma of freshly brewed coffee and the sound of friendly chatter filling the air. She found a cozy corner table and settled in, sipping her latte while lost in her own thoughts. It had been a while since she had seen or spoken to her sister, Kayla, and their relationship had become strained.

As if by fate, Nikki looked up and saw Kayla walking through the door. There was a mixture of surprise and relief on Kayla's face as their eyes met. Nikki couldn't help but notice the tired lines etched on her sister's face, evidence of the burden she had been carrying.

Kayla hesitated for a moment before making her way over to Nikki's table. The sisters exchanged a tentative smile, their emotions tinged with both apprehension and a glimmer of hope.

"Nikki," Kayla said softly as she took a seat opposite her. "I've missed you."

Nikki nodded, her voice filled with a mixture of longing and sadness. "I've missed you too, Kayla. It's been hard not having you by my side during everything that's happened."

Kayla lowered her gaze, her fingers tracing the rim of her coffee cup. "I... I made some mistakes," she admitted, her voice tinged with regret. "I was scared, Nikki. Scared of what the truth would do to you, to us."

Nikki's heart ached as she listened to her sister's words. She could see the pain in Kayla's eyes, the weight of the secrets she had carried, trying to protect her in her own way.

"I understand, Kayla," Nikki said softly, reaching out to place her hand on top of Kayla's. "I know you were trying to do what you thought was right. But keeping those secrets from me... it hurt, Kayla. It made me feel isolated, like I couldn't trust anyone."

Tears welled up in Kayla's eyes as she nodded, her voice barely a whisper. "I'm so sorry, Nikki. I never wanted to hurt you. I was just trying to shield you from the pain and confusion."

Nikki took a deep breath, feeling the weight of their shared pain begin to lift. She knew that forgiveness was the only way forward, the only way to rebuild their bond.

"I forgive you, Kayla," Nikki said, her voice filled with sincerity. "We all make mistakes. What's important is that we learn from them and grow together."

Kayla's eyes widened with a mix of relief and gratitude. "Thank you, Nikki," she whispered, a tear rolling down her cheek. "I don't deserve your forgiveness, but I promise to do better. To be there for you, no matter what."

The sisters shared a moment of understanding, their past grievances slowly dissipating into the air. They knew that rebuilding trust would take time, but they were committed to healing the wounds that had threatened to tear them apart.

As they sat in the coffee shop, talking and laughing like they used to, Nikki realized that their journey toward reconciliation had only just begun. But the most important step had been taken—they had opened their hearts to forgiveness and understanding.

In that moment, surrounded by the comforting ambiance of the coffee shop, Nikki felt a renewed sense of connection with her sister. They were ready to face the challenges ahead, armed with the knowledge that their bond was strong enough to weather any storm.

And as they shared a warm embrace, the wounds of the past slowly began to heal, replaced by the promise of a brighter future together.

Nikki tossed and turned in her bed, her mind restless and filled with a whirlwind of thoughts. Insomnia had returned to haunt her, gripping her in its relentless embrace. She had been plagued by vivid, unsettling dreams that left her gasping for air and drenched in cold sweat. The lines between reality and the horrors of her imagination blurred, leaving her on edge.

As another night passed, Nikki finally gave up on sleep. She swung her legs over the side of the bed and rubbed her temples, trying to soothe the headache that had settled in. Glancing at the clock, she realized it was the early hours of the morning, the world outside still cloaked in darkness.

The house seemed to echo with an eerie silence as Nikki made her way through the dimly lit hallway. She could feel the weight of the past still lingering in every corner, the memories of that fateful night etched into the very walls of her home. She couldn't escape the mess she had left behind, both physically and emotionally.

With each step, the floor creaked beneath her feet, echoing the heaviness in her heart. The house reflected her state of mind—a disarray of scattered belongings, unwashed dishes, and neglected chores. But it was more than just a physical mess. There was something brewing beneath the surface, a storm of emotions threatening to consume her.

Nikki wandered through the rooms, the pale moonlight filtering through the windows and casting long shadows across the walls. She traced her fingers along the dusty surfaces, feeling the weight of her own neglect. The memories of Junior and Mama seemed to haunt her, their presence lingering like ghosts in the very air she breathed.

In the quiet of the night, she closed her eyes, allowing her mind to wander to the twisted visions that plagued her sleep. She saw Junior's menacing stare and Mama's accusing voice, taunting her from the depths of her subconscious. It was a dance between fear and longing, knowing that those figures would never return, yet still feeling their influence in the recesses of her mind.

Her heart raced as she surveyed the chaos around her, realizing that the mess she saw was not just confined to the physical realm. It was a reflection of her inner turmoil, the unspoken emotions she had been avoiding. The events of that night had left scars that ran deep, wounds that had yet to fully heal.

Nikki took a deep breath, the cool night air filling her lungs. She knew that it was time to confront the mess, both inside and outside of herself. It was time to pick up the broken pieces and find a way to rebuild her life, to reclaim her sense of peace and security.

With newfound determination, Nikki set out to clean up her home, one item at a time. As she scrubbed, organized, and restored order, she felt a sense of control seeping back into her life. The physical act of cleaning became a metaphorical cleanse, a way to release the burdens she had carried for far too long.

As the first rays of dawn painted the sky with hues of soft pink and golden light, Nikki stood in her freshly tidied space. The house still held remnants of the past, but she no longer felt trapped within its walls. She knew that healing would take time, but in this moment, she found solace in the small victory of reclaiming her space.

Nikki stood her eyes fixed on the figure she thought she would never see again. George stood at the window, his presence both comforting and unsettling. A wave of emotions surged within her—surprise, disbelief, and a glimmer of hope. Was this real or just another trick of her weary mind?

With cautious steps, Nikki approached the window, her heart pounding in her chest. As she drew closer, George's smile widened, and he waved at her with a warmth that sent a mix of relief and confusion coursing through her veins. She couldn't help but mirror his smile, her eyes welling up with tears.

"George," she whispered, her voice barely audible. But before she could fully process the miracle unfolding before her, a jarring ring pierced the air, shattering the fragile moment of reunion.

Startled, Nikki turned away from the window and hurriedly made her way to the kitchen. Her hands trembled as she reached for the phone, her mind racing with countless possibilities. Who could be calling at this hour, interrupting this precious encounter?

With trembling fingers, Nikki brought the receiver to her ear, her voice strained with a mix of anticipation and anxiety. "Hello?"

A pause hung in the air as if time itself held its breath. Then, a voice—a voice she thought she'd never hear again— spoke from the other end, sending shockwaves through her entire being.

Relief possessed Nikki, an enormous, exquisite relief.

At long last, the longest night was over. There was no more fear to haunt her, no longer a need to steel her nerves against the relentless onslaught of terror. She found herself standing alone in the street, with her thoughts, and her memories, severed from the chaos that had consumed her existence.

Nikki contemplated the significance of it all. Yet, in the grand scheme of things, what did it truly matter? She was alive. She sat there, her weary form, battered and bruised, on the precipice of serenity. The shackles of fear had been cast off, and in their absence, she reveled in the absence of trepidation.

The sun, still distant from its descent, painted the sky with somber hues, gradually enveloping the day in darkness.

Nikki roused herself from her contemplation, finding solace on the sidewalk. A single sentiment consumed her being—an overwhelming sense of finality.

It dawned upon her that she was parched, weary to the bone. Fatigue overshadowed all else, a weariness that seeped into her very soul. All she desired was a soothing shower, a place to rest her weary body and surrender herself to the embrace of slumber. And when the curtains of sleep would finally fall, she longed for the respite of dreams, an oasis of tranquility within her restless mind.

Perhaps, in due time, inquiries would arise, voices inquiring about her whereabouts. Yet, their opinions held little sway over her present state. At this moment, as she stood alone, their thoughts mattered naught. Oh, how she yearned for this solitude!

Stepping off the curb of the bustling downtown street, Nikki glanced out into the world. There was nothing to fear anymore. No sinister secrets lurking in the shadows, poised to strike. Fear, she contemplated, was an invisible force of immense power.

But it was vanquished now, extinguished by her own indomitable resolve and unwavering resilience. She had confronted and conquered her deepest terrors. With each step she took along the lively thoroughfare, she embraced the rising sun, its radiance casting vibrant hues of red and orange across the heavens. Nikki acknowledged the significance of the day unfolding before her.

The soreness that plagued her was overpowering—every muscle ached, her head throbbed incessantly, her mind teetered on the precipice of exhaustion. But there was no cause for fear anymore, no reason to succumb to its insidious grip. It was time to rest, to find respite in the solitude that awaited her. A widow, a woman, she found solace in her identity.

A smile tugged at the corners of her lips as she marveled at the strangely peaceful air that enveloped her. Silence settled, broken only by the approach of a car, its rumbling engine disrupting the tranquility of the street. Nikki's heart fluttered, for she recognized the familiar presence that drew nearer.

"It's you," she whispered softly to herself as she opened the car door and settled into the comforting embrace of the passenger seat. Their eyes met, and a smile illuminated his face. As she allowed her head to sink back against the headrest, a profound realization struck her—she had never truly seen *his* face before. It was his eyes, she mused, his beautiful and familiar eyes that had captured her heart.

"Where shall we go?" he inquired, his voice a gentle caress.

A smile graced Nikki's lips, an echo of profound relief that coursed through her veins.

"Good question... I'm not sure."

He sat beside her at the helm, hands wrapped around the wheel. Then he whispered in her ear.

"Let's just see where the wind takes us, Little Bird."

END.

Made in the USA
Columbia, SC
25 September 2023

23357326R00129